"Your guardian has already safely left."

"*Left?*" Inexplicably, Loraine was stunned by Florian's words. "Left...without a word to me? But I wanted...."

"You wanted to make sure that he and Monsieur Philippe did not meet at any cost," her employer reminded her dryly.

"Yes, of course." She tried to remember how unspeakably important that was. "But...did he *want* to come and speak to me?"

"Very much."

"Oh, I wish you had let him!"

"At the risk of his running into Monsieur Philippe?"

Loraine didn't answer that immediately. She stared at the great designer instead, as though she had recalled or discovered something that had given her a great shock. Then she said, quite irrelevantly, "I didn't look at Philip, after all. I...I looked at Paul."

MARY BURCHELL

is also the author
of the following titles in
HARLEQUIN CLASSIC LIBRARY

The Wedding Dress

MARY BURCHELL

Originally published as Harlequin Romance #813

HARLEQUIN
CLASSIC LIBRARY

TORONTO • LONDON • LOS ANGELES • AMSTERDAM
SYDNEY • HAMBURG • PARIS • STOCKHOLM • ATHENS • TOKYO

Original hardcover edition published by
Mills & Boon Limited 1961
ISBN 0-373-80088-6

Harlequin edition first published April 1964
Golden Harlequin Library edition, Volume XXXI,
published March 1973
Harlequin Classic Library edition published February 1982

Printed in Canada

CHAPTER ONE

IT WAS A PERFECTLY BEAUTIFUL WEDDING. No one was in any doubt about that.

But then it could hardly have been otherwise, Loraine thought as she stood gravely a few paces behind the bride, hoping that her guardian, somewhere in the congregation, found her back view satisfactory.

After all, the bridegroom was the handsome and charming Roger Senloe, the bride his entrancingly pretty and radiant Marianne, and all the bridal dresses had been specially designed and made by the famous house of Florian. No wonder the photographers had crowded round as the bride entered the church and were almost certainly already jockeying for position once more, in readiness for the moment when the procession should reemerge.

Even now Loraine found it difficult to credit that she herself had become part of this magnificent occasion. And try as she would to keep her whole attention on the ceremony, she could not quite prevent her thoughts from wandering over the extraordinary events that had taken place since her father's death six weeks earlier.

It was no use pretending that Loraine and her father had ever been close to each other. Perhaps, she thought with genuine compassion, because he had expended all that was warm and human in him on her pretty young mother, who had died when she was six. In a curious way, she felt no rancor about her father's indifference. It was as though she had known from the very beginning that something in him, too, had died when she was six, and neither he nor she could do anything to revive it.

He was never in the least unkind to her. But he retreated more and more into the historical research that became his sole joy in life, and for long periods at a time he simply ceased to remember that Loraine existed.

It was all the more astonishing, therefore, to discover on his death that in the last weeks of his life he had apparently been greatly concerned about her. Certainly to the extent of appointing a guardian for her and her affairs.

Perhaps one always did that when there was a certain amount of money involved and the recipient was only eighteen. Loraine was not very clear on that point, but at least she wished he had chosen someone a little less problematical than a remote sort of cousin living in Paris.

She had little doubt that the remote cousin profoundly wished that, too. But there was not much that either of them could do about it. At least, they had not found any real solution to the problem yet.

Since he could not at that moment come to England himself, he had summoned Loraine to Paris. And with very little time even to assess the immensity of the change, she had found herself abruptly transferred from the relative seclusion of an English boarding school to the heady atmosphere of Paris in May.

At eighteen, no one is likely to resent that, of course, and Loraine was no exception. From the moment she stepped off the train at the Gare du Nord she was tinglingly aware of a subtle excitement in the air—that shimmer of something in the atmosphere that belongs solely to Paris. It is akin to the bubbles in champagne or moonlight on the water. No one can define it, and no one with a spark of romance can be quite indifferent to it.

There was nothing the matter with Paris as far as Loraine was concerned. The fly in the amber was the cousin.

Not that Paul Cardine was even really a cousin. Just one of those third or fourth removes that occur in many families and are so difficult to work out to their exact degree of relationship. As far as she was aware, they had never met before. But a tall man, with singularly light blue eyes in a thin tanned face, came up to her without hesitation and said, "You're Loraine Darnell, aren't you?"

"Yes. How did you know?" Loraine could not help asking.

"You looked as I expected you to look," he replied coolly, and she was left wondering if there were something foreseeably odd about her, or if he merely wanted to impress her with his clever powers of deduction.

Conversation in the car, on the way from the station, was not exactly flowing. She made one or two gallant attempts to be pleasing and sociable. But either she failed or his thoughts were very much on something else. And after one or two surreptitious glances at his good but rather uncompromising profile, she lapsed into silence.

His home turned out to be an unexpectedly large and luxurious apartment, and here he handed her over to his housekeeper—an elderly woman who answered to the unexpectedly coy name of Mimi. She spoke in the harsh accents of Normandy, which sounded disconcertingly different from any French Loraine had learned at her English boarding school, and she seemed hardly more interested in Loraine than her master was.

It would all have been very dismaying if two English friends of her new guardian had not providentially dropped in for drinks before dinner. These were introduced to Loraine as Roger Senloe, a colleague of Paul Cardine's at the embassy, and Marianne Shore, who was to marry Roger in a fortnight's time.

It was Marianne who got Loraine cozily into a corner and drew her out on the subject of her arrival in Paris, while the two men discussed something of obvious interest to them both.

"Do you mean you have no family at all except Paul Cardine, you poor little thing?" exclaimed the friendly Marianne.

"There are some other cousins of varying degree scattered about England, I believe," Loraine said, "but I don't really know any of them. I don't really know...Paul." It was quite difficult to refer to him thus familiarly when he was such a remote and aloof sort of person. "It's just that my father picked him out as the one most suitable to be a—my guardian. Though I'd much rather he'd chosen some stuffy old family lawyer, to tell the truth," she added under her breath.

"But then you wouldn't have come to Paris," pointed out the sharp-eared Marianne with a smile. "And Paris in May is something not to be dismissed lightly."

"Well, that's true." Loraine could not help smiling, too. "Have you lived here a long time?"

"Not really, no. And after we're married Roger and I are going to Vienna. He's just been transferred there."

"Oh, I'm sorry," Loraine said, very truly. For she had just been thinking what a support this friendly happy girl would be in her new strange life.

"I'm sorry, too, in many ways," Marianne admitted. "Though Roger says Vienna is heavenly. But I'll tell you what I'll do." She looked kindly at the younger girl's slightly disconsolate expression. "I'll see to it that you meet as many of our friends as possible before we go. Then you'll have the nucleus of a circle and.... Why—" She stopped suddenly. "Do you mind standing up for a minute and letting me see how tall you are?"

Slightly mystified, Loraine obliged, and the other girl actually clasped her hands with delight.

"You're just the right height! And dark, too, which is what we need—and so slender and pretty. Oh, Loraine—may I call you Loraine? Will you please do me a great favor?"

"Why, of course—if I can." Loraine was touched and flattered by this appeal, as well as puzzled.

"Will you *please* be one of my bridesmaids?"

"One of your bridesmaids?" Loraine exclaimed, flushing with pleasure and astonishment. "But I—you hardly know me. I mean, it's a sort of...of honor and

privilege to be a bridesmaid, isn't it? Something reserved for family and old friends.''

"But one can have anyone one likes," Marianne
asserted firmly. ''And I'd like to have you.''

"Because you're rather...sorry for me?''

"Oh, no! Nothing horrid and condescending like
that!'' Marianne rejected such an idea scornfully.
"Partly because I liked you on sight, and partly because
it would be of the utmost assistance to me.''

"But how?'' Loraine looked intrigued, and again she
could not help smiling at the vivid face before her.

"I'm unexpectedly one bridesmaid short because an
old school friend has gone and got married herself. I
could just have borne it myself to have the procession
rearranged, but Florian won't hear of it and is in a great
to-do about it.''

"Florian?'' said Loraine questioningly.

"*The* Florian, you know. The great dress designer,''
Marianne explained rapidly. ''He was my employer,
and he and his wife are Roger's closest friends. They
angelically insisted on giving me my wedding here in
Paris. That's why I'm being married here, instead of at
home in England, and my family is coming over for it.''

"But what a princely gesture for an employer to
make!'' Loraine looked astonished.

"Florian's like that. He can be madly generous, and
he enjoys what you aptly describe as princely gestures.
Also, I'm bound to say he likes to be the one to manage
things.'' Marianne smiled indulgently. ''Roger says it's
wonderful publicity for him—but that's Florian, too.
He's the oddest mixture of romance and worldliness.''

"He sounds nice,'' Loraine said.

"Oh, he's a *darling*!'' Marianne declared. ''Usually,'' she added, as though some sharp recollection made
her qualify that. ''And though I really don't mind much
about the details of this wedding, as long as Roger is the
bridegroom, I haven't the heart to question Florian's
arrangements. He's almost personally offended that I'm
one bridesmaid short, and you really would solve a

problem if you would be the substitute. Besides, I'd love to have you," she concluded winningly.

"Then of course I should simply love to accept," Loraine assured her. "But I suppose—" she glanced doubtfully across the room "—I have to ask my cousin first."

"Whatever for?" Marianne wanted to know.

"Well, he's—I suppose he's responsible for me now. I'm sure he would *expect* me to consult him about anything."

"Then I'll ask him." Marianne was evidently sure of her own ability to get what she wanted. "Mr. Cardine?" She raised her voice slightly, and Loraine's cousin immediately glanced across.

"I'm going to borrow Loraine for one of my brides-maids, if you have no objection. Don't you think it's a splendid idea, Roger?" she ran on, as though the matter were already settled. "She is just the right height. Florian will be charmed."

For the first time Loraine saw her guardian smile, and a very attractive smile it was, with a sparkle of genuine amusement for Marianne's tactics, she thought.

"I imagine Loraine will be delighted," he said with a hint of indulgence in his voice that was presumably for Marianne rather than his cousin. "What about getting her dress? There isn't much time left."

"That's just it. Her dress is more or less ready, as it was prepared for someone of almost exactly her build. There'll be hardly any alteration needed. Florian must see her tomorrow."

And so, to Loraine's mingled bewilderment and delight, she had been rushed along the following morning to the famous dress house in the Avenue Georges V. There a slight, charming but authoritative man had pronounced her suitable for the bridal procession, and she found herself one of eight pretty, eager girls who were to follow Marianne to the altar.

As a very latecomer, she felt a trifle diffident about her part in things. But to her surprise she earned the

instantaneous approval of Madame Moisant, the waspish but infinitely efficient *directrice* of Florian. And at
the final fitting, Madame Moisant bluntly told the
others that they could not do better than copy Mademoiselle Loraine in the way they held their heads and in
the matter of general carriage.

"Thus," she assured them, "you will look like
flowers upon a stem rather than camels looking for
water."

Everyone made the utmost effort to look like flora instead of fauna after that, and in the final event,
undoubtedly the bridesmaids would have stolen the
show if the bride had not looked so supremely lovely
and happy. Florian, however, was too good a showman
to allow the principal figure to be eclipsed by mere
supers. And so Marianne remained the center of what
was undoubtedly a ravishing picture.

She looked very grave and sweet, but intensely happy.
And if it had not been for the thought of Philip Otway,
Loraine would almost have envied her—though in the
friendliest and most well-wishing way possible, of
course.

But if one had Philip in the back of one's mind—and
indeed, very often in the front of it, too—it was not
possible to envy anyone who was marrying only nice
Roger Senloe. For Philip was the most romantic, the
most exciting thing that had ever happened in Loraine's
life. He was, in fact, her principal reason for regretting
and even resenting the somewhat arbitrary move that
had taken her from England to Paris.

The Otways—Philip and his elegantly beautiful
mother—had rented the attractive but startlingly
modern house that was the nearest habitation to
Loraine's own rather gloomy home. She had known
nothing about their actual arrival because she had been
away at school. But during the long summer holidays of
the previous year she had first met Philip.

It had been on the day she was eighteen. And even
now, as she stood motionless and apparently absorbed

behind Marianne—her graceful dark head crowned with its wisp of tulle, her dark-fringed gray eyes wide and serious—she trembled slightly to remember the exquisitely sweet importance of that meeting.

He had only said, "Hello, what are you doing here all alone?" But as she had looked up at him from the warm turf on which she was sitting, and noted the strong graceful lines of his figure and the easy way his long brown fingers held his horse's reins, she thought she had never seen anything or anyone who more truly embodied romance.

"I'm doing absolutely nothing," Loraine had informed him rather disconsolately. "And if you want to know, I'm fed up with it."

He laughed at that, and turning his horse loose to graze, he came over and dropped down on the heather beside her.

"Tell me about it," he said, as though it really mattered to him that she was unhappy.

"It's not really very interesting," she began.

But then suddenly, because his laughing dark eyes surveyed her with such interest and understanding, she found herself telling him all about the fact that she was eighteen that day and no one—not even her father—had noticed it.

"You mean, no presents? No party? No anything?" He seemed incredulous. "Oh, but we must do something about that!"

"But how?" Fascinated by the idea that he could possibly interest himself in her little affairs, Loraine had gazed at him as though he were a being from another world.

"Where do you live?" he inquired. "And what is your name?"

She had told him unhesitatingly, and when he discovered that they were, as he put it, practically next-door neighbors, he declared that the whole thing was simple.

"I shall take you home to my mother and we'll make a little party for you," he informed her. "My mother will telephone your father and explain that we're keeping you with us for the evening."

"B-but we're strangers," she stammered. "You don't know anything about me."

"I know a great deal about you," he retorted. "I know that you're called Loraine and you're eighteen and the prettiest sweetest thing I've seen for many a long day. What more do I need to know?"

He had taken her home with him then, and Mrs. Otway proved to be just as charming and kind as her son. She insisted on telephoning to explain Loraine's absence, even though Loraine hardly thought her father would notice her nonappearance, and then both the Otways contrived to impart an enchanting air of festivity to the afternoon and evening.

Incredibly, Mrs. Otway even found a lovely silk scarf for a birthday present. And when he learned that Loraine took ballet lessons and was passionately interested in the subject, Philip Otway produced a beautifully illustrated book on famous ballerinas, from his own collection. He wrote her name in it and the date of her eighteenth birthday, "so that you will never forget the day," as he said.

For other reasons, too, Loraine knew she would never forget that day. For one thing, that was when she fell completely and irretrievably in love with Philip.

She was not entirely aware of this the very first day, of course. But during the rest of the summer the Otways made it their business to see a good deal of the lonely girl on the next estate. And Loraine soon discovered—a discovery only confirmed during the Christmas holidays—that life without Philip and his mother had been no more than a dull existence.

Both of them had been away from home when Loraine had been briefly summoned from school to her father's funeral. And then had come the transfer to Paris. And although it was incredibly exciting and thrilling to be a bridesmaid at a fashionable wedding and wear a Florian creation, Loraine still thought nostalgically of Philip and knew that what she wanted most in the world was to have him smile at her and assure her that somehow he would always be there.

It was difficult to make any firm plans of her own, because her guardian had not yet outlined his ideas for her future. But she cheered herself with the recollection that the Otways came to Paris sometimes, Philip because he was a successful artist and had artistic connections there, and Mrs. Otway because she bought her clothes there—even, Loraine thought she remembered, at Florian's.

So she refused to torment herself with the idea that any real break had taken place. She must be patient— just as one had had to be throughout the terms at school—and presently Philip would be there again and all would be well.

At the reception after the wedding—held in one of the smaller but most exclusive hotels in Paris—Loraine found herself the object of a gratifying amount of admiration.

Even her guardian said to her, "You looked absolutely charming, Loraine." And though she thought it was perhaps more satisfaction at her having done him credit than anything else, she warmed to the smile of approval that he bestowed on her before he went to speak to more interesting people.

Then Madame Florian herself came up to tell Loraine how beautifully she had played her part. And when Loraine ventured to congratulate her shyly on her perfect English, she laughed and said, "But I *am* English, my dear. I was an English model in Florian's dress house. And then he married me."

It sounded deliciously simple and romantic, Loraine thought, put that way, and she looked at Madame Florian with interest.

"Isn't it awfully difficult to get into a French dress house if you're English?" she inquired.

"Not if you have what the designer happens to want."

"And what is that?" Loraine asked with real curiosity.

"Oh—" Gabrielle Florian laughed "—it's difficult to define, and not always just the same quality. There must be a certain amount of grace and...charm, I suppose, and the ability to wear clothes, of course. But over and above that there has to be a subtle something that moves a great designer to fresh inspiration."

"And you have that?" Loraine looked impressed.

"I'm not sure that I have," was the frank reply. "I wasn't a professional model, chosen from a crowd. I was substituted at the last moment for someone who had had an accident a few days before the collection was to open. I think I owed my chance to a fortunate likeness and the right measurements. Then, before I really found my place in the next collection, I married Florian. So we never found out." But she laughed again, on a happy note that suggested she was satisfied to remain in ignorance of her real qualifications since she had achieved her heart's desire instead.

"Then I suppose—" Loraine glanced across at the beautiful bride, now the center of congratulation and admiration "—I suppose Marianne had that indefinable quality you speak of?"

"Oh, no. Not at all, according to Florian himself. She's a lovely charming girl and a perfect darling. But not a designer's source of inspiration. That's something quite different. It's...." Gabrielle gestured a little helplessly, a curiously French movement, to show how impossible it was to explain the inexplicable.

"But Monsieur Florian was Marianne's employer, surely?"

"Oh, yes, of course. But she was in the boutique downstairs. A wonderful saleswoman and a great attraction there."

"I see." Loraine considered that thoughtfully, her wide gray eyes reflective between their smoky dark lashes. "Then I wonder just what—"

"*Mademoiselle*, you played your part very well

today.'' It was Florian himself who had come up unexpectedly to add his word of approval.

"Oh, thank you, *monsieur.*'' Loraine glanced at him shyly. "I tried to walk and stand as Madame Moisant had told us."

"No, no." He shook his head and regarded her with that faint reflective smile that always meant that he was either intensely interested or cleverly hiding the fact that he was bored. "You did nothing so deliberate and tiresome as that. You had completely absorbed Madame Moisant's advice so that you were able to forget about it all when the time came. And quite rightly so. You were thinking of something quite different from the necessity of standing correctly behind the bride, weren't you? That was why your face was interesting."

"Well, I—I.... How did you know, *monsieur?*'' asked Loraine, coloring slightly.

"Because it is my business to know these things,'' Florian replied with a dry little smile. "Of what were you thinking, *petite?*''

"Do I. . . have to tell you?''

"Not necessarily. But I should like to know.''

"Then I was thinking of someone—of two people, I mean—whom I like very much. And I was wondering when I would see him—them again.''

If Florian noticed the two slight corrections—and without doubt he did—he made no sign of doing so. He merely inquired, with an air of kindly interest, "What exactly are you doing here in Paris, *mademoiselle?*''

She thought it was nice of him to inquire so much after her welfare, which was the effect that Florian had on most people when he was finding out something he wanted to know.

"I'm not doing anything specific," Loraine explained easily. "My father died recently and made Mr. Cardine my guardian. As he lives here, the most obvious thing was for me to join him until. . . until it was decided what to do with me.''

She was unaware that a faintly melancholy shade

crossed her face at that point. But the observant Frenchman watching her missed nothing. He said, aside, to his
wife in French, "The face is wonderfully expressive."

Gabrielle looked surprised. So did Loraine, for her
French was quite equal to what Florian had said. And
opening her gray eyes wide again, she said, "Do you
mean *my* face, *monsieur*?"

"Your face, *mon enfant*."

"Is it?" She put up her hand to her cheek in a doubtful, questing little gesture, as though she might almost
be able to feel the quality that Florian had mentioned.

"The movement of the hands, too. You see what I
mean?" Again the Frenchman spoke to his wife, as
though Loraine were a child who would not follow.

"Yes, I think so." Gabrielle looked half doubtful,
half amused. "There's something innocent and touching about her."

"Is that it?" He frowned consideringly. "I don't
know. It's something. . . indefinable."

At this magic word, which had recently taken on such
a very special meaning, Loraine suddenly found her
breath coming rather quickly.

"Monsieur Florian!" Her very pretty speaking voice
ran up onto a slightly higher note in her excitement.
"Are you saying that I have a. . . an indefinable quality
about me?"

"Just so." He nodded almost absently, while obviously pursuing his own line of thought. "And she
walks well and holds herself admirably," he murmured.
Then his tone became brisk and businesslike as he said,
"Tell me, *mademoiselle*, does Monsieur Cardine of the
chilly manner and remote ways intend to maintain you
in comfortable idleness, or do you plan to make your
own living?"

"Monsieur Cardine of the chilly manner and remote
ways," replied Loraine, who liked the description, "is
certainly not going to maintain me in any sense at all. I
don't know yet what my father left—not more than
enough to provide me with a small income, I imagine,

and this Monsieur Cardine—I mean my cousin Paul—will presumably administer for me until I'm twenty-one. But for my own part, I certainly intend to earn my own living, rather than be dependent—''

"Bon!" Florian had heard all he wanted to hear and checked any further development of the theme. "Then I offer you the chance of work in my firm.''

"Monsieur Florian!" She was suddenly speechless.

"You like the idea?" He smiled, that truly wonderful smile that he kept for moments of real kindness or very important business.

"Like it? I love it! Why, I would willingly pick up pins in your dress house if I thought—"

"Not willingly, *mademoiselle*," Florian interrupted with good-humored irony. "It is a tedious and back-breaking job that no one embarks upon willingly. But we will not waste you on that. I need a model for the new collection. We go on show in July, as you probably know, and we have not too much time. But it is decided, then, that you come to me as my youngest model?"

"Why—why, yes, please. At least—I must speak to my guardian first. But I mean to, anyway. Only—oh, please wait one moment while I speak to him."

Loraine darted across the room, threading her way easily and skillfully among the crowds, until she arrived, a trifle breathless, beside Paul Cardine, who was standing by one of the long windows, not engaged in conversation with anyone at that moment.

"Paul...." She actually caught hold of his arm in her eagerness. "Paul, something terribly exciting has happened—"

A laughing group pushed past just then, so that she was pressed quite close against him, and she saw him glance down at her eager flushed face with an almost startled air.

"Oh, I'm sorry...." She suddenly became aware that she was eagerly digging her fingers into his arm, and she also realized surprisedly that it was the first time she had actually touched him. "I didn't mean to grip

you like that, but—do listen! Monsieur Florian wants
me to be a model in his dress house!''

"Florian does?" He looked incredulous. "You must
be mistaken. You're only a child."

"I'm not a child! I'm eighteen," said Loraine indignantly.

"Are you? Well, yes, of course, I remember you
are." He glanced down at her almost somberly then,
and in some queer way, as though he saw her for the
first time. "But that's still awfully young, Loraine, to
be holding your own in such a raffish and competitive
world."

"*Monsieur*, you do my dress house less than justice,"
observed Florian's voice behind her, and she turned
with some relief to see that the great designer had come
to reinforce her own plea. "There is nothing particularly raffish about it, and in many ways it is quite distressingly humdrum and respectable. Behind the scenes, of
course," he added. "The only danger that Mademoiselle Loraine will run will be that of being worked
off her feet."

"Well, that never hurt anyone," observed Paul Cardine with a slight and unexpected smile. And he looked
down at Loraine again and rather absently put his hand
over the fingers that still eagerly gripped his arm. "You
want to do this thing very much, Loraine?"

"Oh, of course! I'm absolutely set on doing it. Only I
thought I would ask—tell you about it first," she added
with belated diplomacy.

He seemed faintly amused by that.

"The rights of a guardian are not very clearly defined, are they?" he remarked dryly.

"Well—" she began doubtfully.

But Florian interrupted to say with frank but quite
friendly curiosity, "Surely, *monsieur*, you are rather
young to be made the guardian of a young girl?"

"Yes, of course. The whole thing is very odd and ir-
regular," the other man agreed, a trifle impatiently. "I
can act as trustee, of course, but as for my being a guar-

dian with any real authority over her, Loraine and I are both uncomfortably aware that the position is untenable and even faintly ridiculous.''

"I wasn't uncomfortable about it," said Loraine, which made both the men laugh. "I mean, I didn't even know that was how you felt about it.''

"Did you think I was at ease in my role?" he inquired dryly, but there was a glimmer of amusement in the blue eyes that looked down at her.

"N-no. At least, I just thought you were completely fed up at having to have me," she explained simply and without rancor.

There was an odd little silence. Then he said, "I'm sorry. I didn't mean to give quite that impression.''

"The air is clearing admirably," observed Florian. "But we still have not settled the point that interests me most. As a guardian or trustee—with or without rights—are you now satisfied, *monsieur*, that Mademoiselle Loraine should work as a model in my irreproachably respectable establishment?''

"I thought Loraine had already decided that and was only pausing to tell me of her decision," replied Paul Cardine a trifle disagreeably.

But on an impulse she could never afterward explain, Loraine quixotically put the whole project in doubt at that point by saying, "I didn't make a decision. I was asking you for your permission." And then she suddenly put her cheek against the arm she was holding and said, "*Please*, Paul.''

There was no mistake about the startled quality of the silence that greeted that. Then he said, "You have my permission." But he gently and determinedly disengaged his arm at that point, and turned away to speak to Roger, who had just come up.

"*Bravissimo!*" remarked Florian, but whether in satisfaction at the general result or amused approval of her technique, Loraine was not quite sure. In any case, it hardly mattered. At the moment all she could take in was the glorious incredible fact that she was to work in the great house of Florian.

"Monsieur Florian, when do I start?" Her flushed eager face and her shining gray eyes made the famous designer smile.

"On Monday. And let me warn you that it is a hard, wearisome, back-breaking job at times. It is not amusing to stand still for hours while I drape and pin material and then change it all and perhaps swear at you."

"Oh, *monsieur*! Are you trying to discourage me now?"

"No, *mademoiselle*. I am merely giving you a healthy reminder that behind all the beauty and glamour of a dress show there is an infinite amount of hard, slogging, unromantic work. When you sit there, watching an apparently leisurely model drift elegantly past—"

"I've never done that," interrupted Loraine. "I've never attended a dress show."

"You've never attended...?" For a moment the Frenchman seemed to glimpse a strange world beyond his ken. "But where have you been, *mon enfant*?"

"At school," said Loraine humbly.

"At school?" repeated Florian, and then he laughed more heartily than was often the case with him. "At school! But how charming! And that, of course, is why you look as you do. I am indeed fortunate."

He patted her cheek sharply but not unkindly.

"There—go now and speak to Marianne, who is signalling to you. Until Monday...." And with a slight pleasant gesture of farewell, he left to rejoin his wife.

Loraine, half charmed and half puzzled by the way he had received the reference to her schooldays, went immediately to Marianne.

"Darling, it's time I slipped away to change," the bride whispered. "I hope I'm not tearing you away from anything that's madly interesting."

"Oh, no. It's all settled, anyway," said Loraine, looking starry-eyed and supremely contented.

"I'll tell you later," Loraine promised as she and

Marianne made their way from the room and then, by private lift, to the bedroom suite that the hotel had put at the bride's disposal.

"It's been wonderful!" Marianne declared as Loraine helped her to lift the beautiful delicate headdress from her head. "I've enjoyed every moment of it. They always say you're too nervous to enjoy your own wedding. But I've adored mine! Dear Florian—it was largely owing to him, I'm sure, that absolutely everything went without a hitch."

"I imagine that everything he undertakes goes without a hitch," said Loraine, carefully unzipping the exquisite dress.

"We-ell, I don't know about that." Marianne stepped out of the incredible cloud of beauty that was her wedding dress. "In the salon itself there can be hitch after hitch, and the first day the collection is shown is usually pure hell. I used to cherish a desire to be a model once. But now I thank heaven I was only in the boutique. Enough can happen there, goodness knows! But oh, the crises, the tears, the intrigues, the jealousies of the salon itself. Why—what's the matter, Loraine? You look...odd, somehow."

"It's nothing," said Loraine bravely, "except that I've just agreed to be a model in Florian's salon."

"Oh, *no*!" Marianne looked dismayed, and then impressed, and then began to laugh in spite of herself. "I say, I'm sorry to have told you such tales, and of course it's the most stupendous compliment to have been chosen like that. Do you mean that Florian just picked you out and offered you the job?"

"Yes. I...I suppose one would describe it like that."

"But, my dear Loraine, how exciting! It's—why, it's the most incredible thing! An absolutely unknown girl—almost a schoolgirl. It's comparable to the time when he rushed Gabrielle in at the last moment, to save his show. And it happened at my own wedding! How lovely!"

And she leaned forward and kissed Loraine, before

slipping into the deceptively simple but entrancing hyacinth blue dress and jacket that Florian had considered proper for her going-away outfit.

"Then you don't think I'm going to have such a harrowing time after all?" Loraine smiled, but there was a shade of anxiety in her tone.

"Well...." Marianne turned from the mirror, her comb in her hand. "I don't know quite what to say to you, Loraine. I don't want to scare you, and yet you're such a child somehow."

"I'm not. I'm eighteen," said Loraine, as she had said to her guardian.

"I know. But there are different *grades* of eighteen. At eighteen, I'm sure Lisette, for instance—" she spoke half to herself "—had forgotten more than you'll ever know."

"Lisette?"

"One of Florian's models. I had trouble with her. She's the kind of girl who makes trouble as a bee gathers honey. It's something between an instinct and a hobby."

"And is she still...there?"

"Oh, yes, of course. She's altogether too unusual and striking for Florian to dispense with her for anything less than murder. And even that he'd hush up if it took place just before opening day," Marianne declared cheerfully. "But just keep to yourself, Loraine, and don't believe more than a third of what anyone tells you and...oh, I suppose you'd better consult your guardian if there's any real trouble."

"Paul? I shouldn't think of going to him if I had any difficulty at work," Loraine declared with some energy.

"No?" Marianne gave her a half amused, half curious glance before turning back to the mirror and running the comb through her hair. "Well, he's straight anyway. And that's more than you can say of some of the people you'll be dealing with."

Loraine was silent, and after a moment Marianne said, "You don't like him, do you, Loraine?"

"I...haven't really made up my mind about him," Loraine confessed. "He was rather nice about my going to Florian's. But he's cold and remote somehow. And he didn't make me feel in the least welcome when I arrived."

"It wasn't a good moment in his life, Loraine."

"W-wasn't it?" Somehow she had never thought of her guardian having personal problems of his own. "How do you mean?"

"Well...." With some deliberation, Marianne poised an exquisitely ridiculous apology for a hat upon her head. "I suppose there's no harm in my telling you. It isn't a breach of confidence because quite a number of people knew about it. And it might give you a more lenient view of him. Only about three days before you came he was chucked for someone else, in rather brutal circumstances, by the girl he was going to marry."

"Oh, Marianne! I'm so sorry," cried Loraine with genuine feeling and sympathy, for she was a tender-hearted girl. "I had no idea."

"No, of course not. You couldn't. And he's the last person to say anything about such a wounding experience. I suppose with anyone like Paul Cardine it's a frightful affront to one's pride as well as one's affections."

"I suppose so," agreed Loraine soberly. "Did you know her, Marianne?"

"Only passingly."

"Did you like her?"

"She wasn't my sort," said Marianne, justly but somehow revealingly.

"And what about him—the other man?"

"I saw him only once," Marianne explained, "but I'm bound to say he was a charmer of the first water. A very good-looking man. An artist called Philip Otway."

CHAPTER TWO

FOR A MOMENT Loraine continued to gaze in speechless dismay at Marianne's back, as the other girl stood before the mirror, adding a last dusting of powder to her charming nose. Then in a stifled sort of voice she said, "Did you say...Philip Otway?"

"Why, yes." Marianne turned swiftly at her tone. "Is there something the matter?"

Loraine did not answer immediately. She simply could not. And Marianne added curiously, almost anxiously, "Do you know him, Loraine?"

"Yes." Loraine nodded, unable to dissemble. "I know him...quite well."

"Then you must have heard about his engagement?"

But Loraine shook her head.

"I haven't seen him—or his mother—for some months," she said slowly. "I had no idea."

"Loraine...." Hurried as she was, as indeed most brides are when about to depart on their honeymoon, Marianne sat down and held out her hand to the other girl. "Loraine, is this especially important to you? I mean, is Philip Otway especially important to you?"

"In a way, yes." Loraine stood there, childishly twisting her hands together instead of taking the hand held out to her. "But—but perhaps only in my mind. There was nothing...." She stopped. Then she said with an effort, "He probably didn't know that I...that I liked him. I wouldn't have told anyone, in the ordinary way, but—"

"You don't need to worry," Marianne assured her. "Your secret's quite safe with me. But if he treated you badly—"

"Oh, it was nothing like that!" Shattered though she was, Loraine felt she must have justice done to Philip. "He wasn't in any way committed to me, Marianne. It was just that he and his mother lived near my home. They were both very kind to me in the holidays. That was all."

She made a touching little gesture of resigned finality that would have charmed Florian and then said, "Would you please try not to think any more about it, Marianne?"

"If that's what you really want." Marianne looked doubtful, but she stood up once more, as though she had suddenly remembered her own affairs.

"That's what I really want," Loraine insisted bravely. And she even managed to smile a little as she helped Marianne to complete her final preparations and then accompanied her back to the reception room once more.

Everyone crowded around. There was a great deal of kissing and congratulation. For a moment Marianne clung to the two pleasant-looking, middle-aged people Loraine knew to be her parents. Then there was a kiss for the Florians before, suddenly catching each other by the hand, Marianne and Roger ran out to the waiting car, almost before anyone could realize what was happening.

The guests made a concerted rush to the side exit of the hotel; there was a spatter of applause and even a few cheers. Then the car slid away and everyone straggled back into the hotel, with that strange deflated feeling that occurs at every wedding after what someone has tellingly called "the point of no return."

About half the company set about leaving almost immediately. Some of the others stood about for a short while longer, sipping Florian's excellent champagne and exchanging final comments on the wedding. But then they, too, began to drift away, and presently Loraine's guardian came up and said, "Shall we go now?"

"Yes, if you like."

As they moved over to say goodbye to their host and

hostess, she could not help glancing at Paul Cardine and seeing him in an entirely new light. Not only as someone who had received a blow curiously similar to her own, but also—incredibly—as Philip's rival.

Their thanks and goodbyes said, they turned to go. But, as they did so, Florian said to Loraine, "Monday morning, *mademoiselle*—at nine o'clock. Report to Madame Moisant, please."

"Yes, *monsieur*!" Loraine spoke quickly and obediently over her shoulder, already as one addressing not her host but her employer. And then she followed Paul out to his car reflecting—as many had before her—on the extraordinary talent Florian possessed for creating the exact atmosphere he required.

In the car she had a sudden and crazy impulse to ask her guardian something about his broken engagement. She suppressed it immediately, of course, for she simply could not imagine herself really talking to him on any personal matter. And yet, here, sitting beside her, was one of the few people who could presumably have told her quite a lot about the one subject she was burning to discuss.

She wondered if he hated Philip. It was difficult to see how he could do otherwise. And then, in what circumstances had it all happened? Marianne had spoken of a "brutal" break. Possibly that meant that Paul had never even met his rival. He might simply have been presented with a fait accompli by a girl who had changed her mind and was ruthlessly determined to make that clear.

Not that one could blame her in a way, Loraine thought reluctantly. What did one *do* if one were engaged to Paul Cardine and Philip came along? She knew what she would have done—what she would simply have had to do. Only it was desperately hard to be the one who lost.

Again she glanced at Paul, and at that moment he said, "You've very quiet, Loraine. Are you tired?"

"Oh, no!" she assured him. "Not a bit. I enjoyed it all."

"Did you?" He smiled faintly. "But, even so, one feels rather flat after a wedding. Unless one is one of the principals, when I suppose it's different." He curled his lip very slightly. "Would you care to come out somewhere this evening?"

It was the first time he had made any such suggestion, and she was so surprised that she immediately countered with, "Would *you* like that?"

"I'm giving you the choice," he reminded her. "There's a gala performance at the opera, if that interests you."

"Why, of course it does!" She caught her breath on a gasp of ingenuous delight. "But would you be able to get tickets at this late hour?"

"I got tickets several weeks ago when it was first announced," he said flatly. "I intended to take someone else."

"Oh...." Somehow Loraine contrived to hide her keen awareness of what this meant and summoned a brilliant smile. "If I'm not doing anyone else out of a great treat, I should simply love it. Only—" she suddenly looked dashed "—I don't know if I've got anything suitable to wear."

"You can wear what you have on—without the headdress. You could hardly look lovelier," he told her quite impersonally.

"Oh, thank you." For some reason or other, she felt herself blush. "Yes, of course. I forgot I had this heavenly dress. I'll wear it, as you say, and we'll go and it will be wonderful."

"Let us hope so," he agreed as they drew up before his home. And, although his tone was not enthusiastic, it was not exactly unkindly, either.

Loraine made no secret of her eager anticipation as they dined together. In this way, she felt, she might perhaps help to reduce the bitterness of his inevitable reflection that he had originally planned the evening in a very different light. It was his fiancée, not his insignificant ward, he had visualized with him in the happy days before he had any idea of what was going to hit him.

In trying to make the occasion less painful for him, she even succeeded in thrusting her own unhappiness to the outer rim of her consciousness. She did not forget Philip for one single instant. But at least she held off the final and agonizing realization of her loss until she should be alone with no guardian—not anyone—to stand between her and the bleak truth.

Paul was not very talkative as they drove to the opera. But then that was not his way, in any case. He was, however, both amused and pleased by Loraine's wholehearted delight at the sight of the immense red carpet that had been laid not only down the famous center staircase but also right down the steps outside the building.

"I never saw anything like it!" she gasped.

"The French do this sort of thing supremely well," he conceded as, in the brilliant glare of floodlights, they mounted the steps together. And when they finally entered the great building, Loraine caught her breath afresh at the sight of flowers banked in extravagant profusion on every side, while among the elegant crowds who were slowly making their way up the grand staircase, she saw dresses and furs of a beauty and splendor she had never imagined before.

To Loraine—who had been born too late to know the wonderful days when "a well-dressed house" was the natural order of things—it seemed that the scene was fascinating enough even before the curtain went up. And seated in a box beside her guardian, she leaned forward eagerly to study the dresses and jewelry of the women and the splendid orders worn by some of the men.

She was just about to sit back at last with a sigh of pure contentment, when suddenly she felt the blood rush into her face and then away again. Her gaze became riveted on a box that was just within her range of vision if she leaned forward. Two people had entered even as her gaze came idly to rest there. The girl was tall and fair and supremely elegant. The man was Philip.

For a moment she hardly dared to move lest she should betray to Paul that something of enormous significance had just happened. Then, with deliberately controlled leisureliness, she sat back, slightly rearranged her wrap and glanced casually at her guardian.

He was not looking at her. He was also leaning slightly forward, and one glance at his set mouth and grim jawline was sufficient to tell her that he, too, had seen the couple in the circle of boxes below them.

That's the girl, of course! thought Loraine. *It's as much of a shock for him as for me. At least, I suppose it is. Or did he expect her to be here? Was that why he wanted to come, even though it must be a horribly empty occasion for him?*

The lights began slowly to dim at this point and her guardian—reluctantly, she thought—sat back in his seat once more. The conductor had entered. The gala was about to begin.

In the ordinary way, Loraine would have been fascinated by the performance and lost to all outside considerations. But tonight the outside considerations, incredibly, included Philip—in circumstances impossible to ignore.

Until she had that one brief glimpse of him she had been desperately pretending to herself that, if she never saw him again, she could perhaps somehow relegate him to the beautiful nostalgic past. He would become a loved but lost figure who had nothing to do with the exciting challenging life thrown open to her by Florian's astounding offer.

But now she *had* seen him. And she had realized instantaneously that there was no dismissing him as a loved figure of the past. He was terribly and overwhelmingly of the present. But, in all that mattered, she had already lost him to the fair, cool, lovely girl beside him.

Despair engulfed her, even as the music from the orchestra engulfed her. And then she found herself wondering if her guardian were pursuing a similar line of thought. Was he also bitterly accepting the fact that defeat had really been inevitable from the moment that Philip and that girl came together?

She stole a glance at him in the light from the stage. But it struck her immediately that he did not look at all like someone who was accepting defeat as inevitable. On the contrary, his expression suggested grim determination rather than despair. And for the first time since Marianne had stunned her with the news of Philip's engagement, the idea crossed Loraine's mind that perhaps the last word had not yet been said.

Suppose her guardian were *not* prepared to accept defeat? Suppose he thought—and was correct in his belief—that he could get his fiancée back again? What then?

It seemed faintly mean even to think along these lines when Philip had looked so radiantly happy. But *supposing* it all fell out that way, then the first and most obvious result would be that Philip would be left in sad need of consolation.

The idea excited her so powerfully that she made a slight involuntary movement, and her companion glanced at her. But she managed to go on looking at the stage with an air of great attention. And presently the curtain fell on the first act.

In the interval she eagerly accepted her guardian's suggestion that they should go out. But the moment they had left the shelter of the box, she realized that she was being foolishly rash. For however much she might long to see Philip, to see him in company with Paul would be disastrous.

Once he realized the connection, Philip could only be highly embarrassed and would probably avoid her thereafter. While Paul, for his part, might even take a high hand and, with what guardianly rights he might have, forbid her to see Philip again.

She could not quite imagine her guardian doing such a thing—nor herself submitting if he tried it—but, in any case, whatever she hoped for the future would most certainly be jeopardized by a meeting of all the parties at this point.

In spite of her anxiety, however, the interval passed safely, and they returned to the box unidentified. Determined not to run any further risks, Loraine devoted her whole attention to the stage during the next act and, even when the curtain fell once more, she firmly refused to accompany her guardian when he explained that he had promised to meet a colleague during the second interval.

"You go," she urged him. "I'm perfectly happy watching the audience." And the moment he had left her side she leaned forward eagerly in the hope that she might be able to look at Philip for several undisturbed minutes.

Luck was with her. He was alone in the box, standing looking down into the stalls, where his fiancée was talking animatedly to an elderly but very elegant woman.

Loraine lost all awareness of anyone or anything else. In all her meetings with Philip she had not, of course, ever been able to gaze at him in uninhibited delight, noting every line and plane of his handsome interesting face. Now she could—in the blissful certainty that he had no idea she was within a hundred miles of him.

In spite of everything a sigh of complete happiness escaped her. And, at that moment, as though he had actually heard that faint breath of a sound, he moved sharply and looked straight up at her. There was not the smallest chance of concealment. Their glances met with an impact that was almost physical, and she saw his lips form the word, "Loraine!" And then he turned and was out of his box in a flash.

He was coming up to her—of that there was no doubt. And for a moment of sheer joy nothing else mattered. Not the risk of her guardian's return, nor the necessity of making awkward explanations, nor the fact that she was totally unprepared to deal with either contingency. Philip was coming at last.

She stood up when she heard his knock, and as he

entered she turned to him with her hands out. Then everything else in the world was forgotten as he took hold of her lightly, kissed her on both cheeks and exclaimed, "Darling child! What a wonderful surprise. What on earth are you doing here?"

"I'm living in Paris now." She could not stop looking at him and smiling with sheer joy. "My father died. I expect you heard."

"Yes. I'm terribly sorry, my dear. We were abroad, as you probably know. Otherwise we would at least have been with you for the funeral. We didn't hear until two or three weeks afterward."

"And then I was probably already here."

"But how come, Loraine? Good heavens, how lovely you're looking, child! I've never seen you in a more becoming dress."

"It's a Florian," she said simply.

"Well, that explains it." He laughed. "But it doesn't explain everything else. You're not living on your own here in Paris, are you?"

"Oh, no. Not at the moment." She must be careful now, she told herself. She must be terribly careful. "I had—my father had a sort of cousin living here. He was made my guar—trustee. So it was thought best that I should come here for the time being. But I expect I'll be on my own soon, because something wonderful happened. I've been offered a job. Florian has taken me on as one of his models."

"*Florian* has? Loraine, you keep me gasping! You were a retiring schoolgirl when I last saw you. Now I find you a lovely self-possessed young creature, talking of working with the greatest designer in Paris. What has happened to you?"

"N-nothing." She smiled shyly, for she did not feel at all self-possessed, whatever he might say. "I'm not any different, really, Philip."

"You're just as sweet as ever, certainly." He took her hand again and kissed it lightly. "We must get together, darling. Where can I phone you?"

For a moment she felt as though a gulf opened in front of her. And then, on an inspiration born of necessity, she heard herself say quite coolly, "You'd better phone me at Florian's. I—I might be changing my home number soon."

"Very well. In a day or two." He glanced down into the stalls again and made a slight answering sign to the girl who had just glanced up. "I must go now."

With difficulty she suppressed a pang of passionate jealousy. But she also reminded herself that it was time he went, in any case. Her guardian might return at any moment now.

"Goodbye, dear Loraine. That's my fiancée down there, by the way, but there isn't time to tell you all about her now. We'll cover the rest of the news over lunch some time soon, and mother will be here in a week or two. I suppose she'll be coming to your opening show. She usually does the Florian opening."

He held her hand tightly for a moment in the special clasp that she knew so well. Then he was gone, and Loraine went slowly back to her seat, feeling dazzled and faintly giddy, like someone who had been looking into the sun too long.

She sat there very still, savoring the memory of every moment he had been there. And she knew that nothing—not her father's death, nor the move to Paris, nor Florian's incredible offer—could compare in importance with the fact that she had seen and talked to Philip once again.

He had said she was lovely and no longer a schoolgirl, too, which must mean that he saw her in a new light. Perhaps it was not only to her that the meeting had been of significance. Again she felt guiltily that one must not pursue such a line of thought since he appeared to be completely and happily committed to someone else. But it was impossible not to bask in the knowledge of his undoubted approval and interest.

Just as the lights were going down once more, Paul slipped back into his seat.

"I'm sorry. I didn't mean to leave you so long," he said. "I hope you weren't bored."

"No," Loraine assured him gently. "I wasn't in the least bored."

"You're a good undemanding child," he remarked unexpectedly. And she found herself wondering guiltily if he would have been quite so sure of that if he had known who had visited the box in his absence.

When it was all over he took her straight home, saying that her day had been long and exciting enough already, but that on some other occasion he would take her out to supper at Maxim's.

She was grateful—and surprised—at the half promise. But she was genuinely glad to go home now. And she was not sorry that the next day, Sunday, proved quiet and uneventful. With the challenge of her first day at Florian's looming near, she was going to need all her energy and freshness.

On the Monday morning she breakfasted early with her guardian, who seemed slightly amused by the fact that her enthusiasm had not wilted before an early rising and the inevitable nervous strain of the first day at any job.

"I hope it's all going to be as enthralling as you seem to expect," he remarked a trifle dryly. "They say Florian is a very hard taskmaster."

"That's just because he's a perfectionist." Loraine's tone held a note of near reverence that would have amused, but not displeased, the great designer. "I don't in the least mind working hard, if I can really be part of that wonderful enterprise."

"Well, that's the right spirit." Her guardian gave her an unexpected grin of sheer amusement that made him look very much younger. "Far be it from me to encourage anyone to give any job less than a fair trial. But I think you have a right to know at this point, Loraine, that you're not entirely dependent on what you can earn."

"How do you mean?"

"Your father's affairs haven't been settled yet, but he certainly left you enough to bring in a small income. In addition—" he slightly moved one or two things on the breakfast table in front of him and, if she had not known it was impossible, she would have thought he was nervous "—you do understand that you're really very welcome here, don't you?"

She opened her eyes rather wide. "It's very nice of you to say so—"

"Well, I was a good deal taken aback to find you thought I was—fed up was, I think, the term—at having to take you in."

"But weren't you?" She smiled at him without rancor and even with a touch of mischief.

"No." He colored very slightly, which astonished her. "I was surprised and a bit nonplussed, I suppose. And—although you were not to know this, of course—it so happened that I had a personal crisis to deal with at the same time."

"I'm very sorry," she said gently. "I hope it has—solved itself now."

"Not exactly. But I take a good deal of convincing that I'm beaten." Again he gave that quick unexpected smile. "In any case, it has nothing to do with the present discussion. I just want to have it quite clear that I don't in any way resent your being here."

"You couldn't really have been blamed much if you had," Loraine told him candidly. "I was simply wished on you out of the blue, and if you had resented me—"

"I didn't and I don't," he asserted categorically. "I'm not sure that I know much about managing a girl of your age—or even how to learn to do so—but you are welcome in my home until you choose to go elsewhere."

He stood up then, as though finishing the discussion. But Loraine got up, too, and came around to him.

"Thank you very much." She put her hand lightly on his arm. "And in any case—" once more her smile had a glint of mischief "—you don't need to learn how to manage me. I've always understood that it's the ward who manages the guardian."

"Is that so?" He gave her cheek a slight but not unkindly pat. "I can't promise that you'll find me very manageable, Loraine. And now it's time you started for work. Do you want me to drive you down?"

"No, of course not! Working girls don't arrive in private cars. I'll walk. It's not far and it's a wonderful morning."

"All right. Goodbye and good luck," he said, and he gave her a casual little nod of something between dismissal and salute.

As Loraine left the tall handsome house in which her guardian's apartment was, she felt her spirits rise with a bound. For the first time in her life, she was setting out toward independence and perhaps adventure—and she was walking there through the streets of Paris on a magical June morning.

The traffic streaming past, the hurrying crowds, the green of the trees on the avenue, the incredible variety of lovely things displayed in the shop windows—all contributed to the feeling of enchantment. And, as though this were not enough, Philip was in the same city.

To others this might be a Monday morning like any other Monday morning. To Loraine it was the most exciting day of her life. And when she came at last to the famous dress house, with the one word, FLORIAN, splashed in letters of gold across the smooth stone of its austere facade, she felt she stood upon the threshold of romance.

However, as it was now five minutes to nine, there was no question of lingering sentimentally upon that threshold. So she entered instead and inquired shyly for Madame Moisant.

Immediately she was wafted up the famous staircase to the small, thickly carpeted room where the *directrice* of Florian's sat at a deceptively simple and austere-looking desk. This, in Madame Moisant's opinion, was the nerve center of the whole great enterprise, and Florian himself would have hesitated to deny it.

She had evidently been informed of Florian's unexpected appointment and, as Loraine knocked diffidently and entered, the Frenchwoman looked up and said, "Come in, *mademoiselle*, and sit down."

It was an order rather than an invitation, and in an instant Loraine was subtly informed that she had exchanged the status of a customer for that of a very junior employee.

She sat down; there was a slight and curiously telling pause. Then the *directrice* said, "*Mademoiselle*, you are about to become part of the greatest dress house in Paris—which is to say in the world. You probably imagine that this opens a prospect of glamour and gaiety, a life in which one does little but wear beautiful clothes and make other women envious."

It had not really been part of Loraine's hopeful expectations to make other women envious, but she hardly liked to correct Madame Moisant on so minor a point. She therefore murmured that she knew she was very fortunate to have been chosen for this position but that she expected to work extremely hard.

"Fine words," agreed Madame Moisant, though in a tone that implied they buttered no parsnips. "You will do well to remember them, *mon enfant*, when you have to model beachwear in the winter and furs in the summer, and above all when you have to stand for hours while Monsieur Florian drapes and designs and redesigns, until your head aches and your arches feel they will never be the same again. This is all part of the romantic—" she curled her lip "—world of the fashion model. It is only just that I should tell you this now."

"Thank you, *madame*," said Loraine, since another telling pause seemed to indicate that gratitude was due for this somewhat depressing preview of her job.

"*Bon!* Then we understand each other." Madame Moisant rose from behind her desk. "You shall now come and meet your other colleagues."

Loraine was not at all sure that they understood each other. But she meekly followed in the wake of the energetic *directrice* and was conducted to a big bare room behind the salon, where half a dozen girls in various stages of undress were either sitting before the long wall mirror making up or disposed about the room in attitudes of complete relaxation.

With one exception, even the relaxing ones came to some sort of attention as Madame Moisant entered and announced briskly, "This is your new colleague, Mademoiselle Loraine. Monsieur Florian has chosen her to model some of the more *jeune fille* numbers in the new collection."

"I thought *I* was to model those."

The one girl who had shown—or feigned—indifference at their entry now raised a beautiful red-gold head from the fashion paper she had been studying and stared with a faint touch of insolence at Madame Moisant.

"Then you thought incorrectly, Lisette," replied Madame Moisant with monumental calm. But the name Lisette awoke uneasy recollections in Loraine's mind, for this, she remembered, was the girl Marianne had described as dangerous.

A sullen cloud descended on the features of the redhead, and her curiously attractive green eyes narrowed like a cat's in the sun.

"Monsieur Florian promised me—" she began.

"Monsieur Florian is not so naive as to promise any one of you anything," cut in the *directrice* with good-humored cynicism. "He knows how much you would then snatch. As soon would he offer his finger to a boa constrictor."

Everyone except Lisette looked somewhat impressed by this grisly simile.

"You have plenty of designs to model, Lisette, without making trouble over the designs of others," Madame Moisant went on, still in that brisk astringent manner. "Loraine was picked out by Monsieur Florian himself for her part at Marianne's wedding."

"Why, yes, of course! You were one of the bridesmaids, weren't you?'' exclaimed a charming, rather impudent-looking little blonde, who turned to Loraine with a friendly smile. "It was beautiful, the wedding, eh?"

"It was lovely." Loraine smiled shyly in return.

"We all liked Marianne and wished her well," declared the blonde kindly.

"I did not wish her well," stated Lisette categorically. But to Loraine's surprise, no one seemed to take much notice of this somewhat embarrassing remark.

"Now I shall leave Loraine with you, Clotilde." With faultless acumen, Madame Moisant now handed over Loraine to the care of the friendly blonde. "You will show her where to put her things and how to conduct herself on this first day. Later it will be decided if she is to wear any of Julie's numbers in the present collection."

"Who is Julie?" inquired Loraine, as Clotilde good-humoredly began to instruct her in the day-to-day running of the models' room.

"She was our youngest model. She left a week ago, also to get married. Monsieur Florian was very angry."

"Why?" asked Loraine, who had not noticed any special antipathy to marriage on Monsieur Florian's part.

"We had not finished the showing of the present collection," Clotilde explained, as though to a child. "It is very difficult to show a design on another model. It was very wrong of Julie, since her husband wished her immediately to leave with him for Australia."

"What ought she to have done, then?" inquired Loraine, half amused and half impressed by the other girl's gravity.

"She should have *waited*," was the simple reply. "The collection must come first."

"I see," said Loraine, somewhat sobered by this first introduction to a scale of values entirely new to her.

During the next half hour most of the girls were called away at various times, either to be fitted for designs in the new collection or to display something for private customers, Clotilde explained. Finally Clotilde herself was summoned and, to her secret embarrassment and even faint alarm, Loraine was left alone with Lisette, who still sat in her corner, her feet up on another chair, apparently absorbed once more in her fashion paper.

Loraine seated herself before the mirror and pretended to do some running repairs to her very simple makeup. But presently, in the glass, she saw the other girl lay down her paper and look across.

There was something indescribably disconcerting in the knowledge that one was being studied by those catlike green eyes, and Loraine actually felt the short hairs at the nape of her neck lift. Then Lisette said without preamble, "I remember now. I saw you on Saturday."

"At Marianne's...at the wedding?" asked Loraine doubtfully.

"No. At the opera gala. You were in a box with a very good-looking man."

"Oh!" Loraine smiled slightly at this description of Paul, though she supposed it was strictly accurate. "That was my guardian."

There was a slight pause. Then Lisette said, "Who was the other man?"

"The...other man?" Loraine met the thoughtful stare of those green eyes in the mirror, and at the same moment it was exactly as though a danger signal flashed a warning in her own mind.

"Yes," said Lisette. "The man who came in and kissed you when your guardian wasn't there."

CHAPTER THREE

A WAVE of quite illogical panic swept over Loraine as Lisette asked that mock innocent question about Philip, and it was only with an effort that she reminded herself there had been absolutely nothing wrong in her meeting with him, however much Lisette's tone might imply there had. It was merely that Loraine would not have liked Paul to know anything about it.

There was probably no more than a second's pause before she said in a steady voice, though not quite accurately, "That was an old family friend, if you must know."

"He didn't kiss you like an old family friend. He kissed you like a lover," stated Lisette, contriving to give the last word a slightly questionable flavor.

"You are mistaken." Loraine spoke firmly and coldly, though secretly she felt a sort of frightened elation that anyone—even Lisette—should find such a quality in Philip's attitude toward her.

Lisette laughed slightly, probably because she was aware that she had disconcerted the other girl.

"You didn't tell your guardian about it when he came back, though, did you?" she said. And once more Loraine felt an irrepressible little thrill of panic at the almost uncannily complete knowledge that this strange inimical girl seemed to have about her.

However, with resolution and quite admirable calm, she said, "I can't imagine why you should take so much interest in my very ordinary affairs. But whatever your efforts, you couldn't possibly have been in a position to know what I said or did not say to my guardian or anyone else. Where were you anyway?"

"I was selling programs."

"Selling programs?" Loraine looked mystified.

"Yes. It was part of the gala atmosphere that the program girls should be supplied—and dressed—by the great fashion houses. I did not want to go. Opera bores me inexpressibly," stated Lisette simply. "But Monsieur Florian insisted. And so I was there, with nothing to do after I had sold my programs except to look round. And then I saw you and knew from your dress that you must have been one of Marianne's bridesmaids."

"I see." It gave Loraine the most uncomfortable feeling to realize that during most of the evening at the opera gala she had been under the scrutiny of those unfriendly green eyes. "Well, I'm afraid I couldn't have provided much antidote to your boredom."

"On the contrary. It is interesting to see a girl arrive in the company of one good-looking man and then, in his absence, throw herself into the arms of another."

"I did *not* throw— Oh, look here, this is all dreadfully silly!" Loraine turned at last from the mirror to face Lisette. "I could tell you to mind your own business, but I don't want to start by being unfriendly to a colleague. I must say, though, it's too absurd of you to try to give some sort of guilty significance to a perfectly ordinary incident. I hadn't seen...the other friend for quite a while. Then, to our complete surprise, we saw each other, though I suppose you noted that, too, if you had me under such complete observation," added Loraine sarcastically.

"No, this I missed," conceded Lisette with naive candor.

"Too bad," said Loraine dryly. "He rushed up to greet me, and we not unnaturally kissed. That's all."

"But you didn't tell your guardian, did you?"

There was something frightening about the way Lisette kept unerringly—and with such confidence—to what was really the crux of the matter. Loraine would have given anything to be able to laugh the whole thing off or to resolutely refuse to answer any more questions. But something in that speculative glance froze any laughter at the source and made one feel that almost any reply would be better than silence, since silence could be interpreted as dangerously as one pleased.

By nature Loraine was a truthful girl, but it took her only a second to decide that, if a curt fib were the only thing to end this most distasteful discussion, then she was prepared to tell it.

"There's no earthly reason why I should answer your silly and inquisitive questions," she said shortly. "But, since you seem so passionately interested, of course I told my guardian of my unexpected visitor."

"When?" inquired Lisette, with the simple scorn of one who could as easily add, "Liar."

"When?" repeated Loraine, unaccountably put out. "How do you mean—when? When he came back into the box, of course. I told him all about my unexpected visitor and he—"

The other girl laughed slightly, and it was an oddly disquieting sound that had the effect of drying up Loraine's fount of eloquence.

"You should have said, 'On the way home,'" Lisette informed her contemptuously. "That no one could have questioned. But me, I know quite well that you did not tell him 'all about' anything when he returned to the box, for the curtain went up almost immediately, and you had time only to exchange half a dozen words. Therefore you did not tell him, but you would like to make out that the handsome guardian is in your confidence when in fact he is not."

Loraine was struck dumb. Partly with the chagrin that descends on any truthful person caught out in the unfamiliar lie. Partly with sheer dismay at the discovery that she had been made to give an air of guilty concealment to something she greatly wished to pass off as natural and unimportant.

Lisette, for her part, looked quite disproportionately pleased at having trapped a virtual stranger into what she evidently considered a damaging admission. That anyone should find satisfaction in such a pointless bit of spite was in itself so baffling to Loraine that she could find no words. And then, as she stared angrily at Lisette, wondering what on earth to say next, a summons came for her to go to Monsieur Florian himself.

Almost running in her desire to get away from Lisette's unwelcome company, she hastened to the top of the building, where Monsieur Florian had his own office and workroom. Here she found him and Madame Moisant in consultation.

"Come in, *petite*," Florian bade her indulgently.

And Loraine—who did not yet know that the great designer ruled his subordinates by a clever mixture of kindness and brutality—thought how lucky she was to have such an employer and that, after all, Lisette and her spiteful ways were of little account.

"We were discussing where—or, indeed, if—we should place you in the present collection," Florian informed her. "It is a question of substituting you for one of my models who has...deserted." The faint pause before the last word conveyed the enormity of the erring Julie's offense to Loraine more clearly than anything Clotilde had said. "Some of her numbers we have already allotted to one or other of the girls. But perhaps—" He turned to Madame Moisant abruptly and said, "Try her in Number Fourteen."

So Loraine was whisked off to a nearby dressing room and, at great speed, arrayed in a deceptively simple little black suit that somehow made her feel like a princess, slightly but charmingly disguised for the purpose of some wistfully romantic adventure. A white hat, which looked innocent in the hand but provocative on the head, completed the outfit and, still under Madame Moisant's close surveillance, she was conducted back to Florian's workroom and instructed to walk to the end of the room and back.

She did as she was told, indescribably intrigued by the

mood that the very wearing of the suit seemed to inspire in her.

Now, if she really *were* a princess escaping from formality and ceremony for a day—perhaps only a precious hour—just so would she dress, thought Loraine. And then anything could happen! Particularly here in Paris. Why—

"Do that again," said Florian's voice, with a curious note of amused attention in it.

So she recalled where she was and obediently retraced her steps. But it was difficult not to revel still in the role of the little princess in disguise, and she only descended completely to earth again when she heard Madame Moisant exclaim a trifle disparagingly, "She does not wear it in the least as Julie wore it."

"No," said Florian softly, "she wears it as only she herself would wear it. She gives it an entirely new identity. Strange. I have seen that happen only about three times before in my life." And then, to Loraine, "Of what were you thinking, *petite*, as you walked up and down my workroom?"

"Well...." She glanced shyly at Florian and blushed. "I was pretending—I mean—" the blush deepened "—Oh, it sounds so silly!"

"Tell me nevertheless," said Florian in the tone he used for drawing large orders out of difficult customers.

"I had the feeling...." Loraine laughed softly and ran her hands gently over the slim lines of the magical suit. "I had the strange feeling that I was a princess, a little bit disguised, and that something touching and...romantic might happen at any minute. Like a fairy story, only in real life. I'm afraid you must think me dreadfully childish! It was only a moment of make-believe and—"

"Try her in all Julie's numbers this afternoon," said Florian, turning to Madame Moisant.

"All of them?" His *directrice* sounded faintly scandalized. "Do you mean those that have already been allotted to Lisette and Clotilde?"

"All of them," repeated Florian coolly. "I want to see what she makes of them."

"There will be trouble," muttered Madame Moisant. "Not with Clotilde, who is philosophical and also lazy. But with Lisette, who is ambitious and envious and fights for every design like a dog for a bone."

"I do not run my business to please Lisette," said Florian dryly. "Loraine will wear all Julie's designs at the show this afternoon. And do not look so solemn, *ma chère*." For a moment Loraine thought he was still addressing Madame Moisant, and then she realized that he had turned to her. "In this world one cannot be both successful and popular. This I have found for myself long ago. To be hated is often the full measure of one's success."

He looked remarkably cheerful about this regrettable state of affairs. So Loraine smiled and also tried to look as though she did not in the least mind being hated, as long as she won his approval.

"Come, then. We have a great deal to do," said Madame Moisant brusquely, as though Loraine were lingering unnecessarily. And once again Loraine was whisked off, divested of her black suit and, when reclothed in her own things, taken down to the salon, where Madame Moisant put her through her paces with regard to the matter of actually appearing in public.

In her sharp astringent way, the Frenchwoman was not unhelpful, and it became perfectly obvious to Loraine that there was nothing—literally nothing—that she did not know about the display and sale of beautiful clothes.

Humbly glad to be instructed by such an expert, Loraine paid the utmost attention to all she was told and tried hard to remember her instructions, at the same time making them sufficiently part of herself to avoid either stiffness or anxiety.

"You have a natural talent," Madame Moisant admitted grudgingly at last. "Well, we will see."

Back in the dressing room, she made the general

unequivocal statement that Loraine would wear all
Julie's designs at the afternoon show.

"What a relief!" exclaimed Clotilde characteristically. "I shall now at least be able to breathe between
appearances."

But Lisette, equally characteristically, cried, "She
shall not wear Fourteen nor Fifty-one. These are mine!
They are *my* models."

"On the contrary, Lisette." It was Florian himself
who, unexpectedly, spoke from the doorway. "They
happen to be my models, and I will decide who wears
them."

"But, *monsieur*—" Lisette was only mildly abashed
"—you promised me—"

"You are mistaken, Lisette. According to my in-
variable custom, I promised you nothing," Florian
assured her courteously. "Loraine will wear Julie's
models this afternoon, and I shall be there myself to see
the show."

From the silence that greeted this last statement,
Loraine gathered it was unusual for Florian himself to
attend the daily dress show so late in the season. And
she was both alarmed and gratified to realize that she
herself must be the reason for his unwonted appearance.

"Afterward," Florian went on calmly, "I shall need
you in my workroom, Lisette. It is possible—though by
no means certain—that I shall use you for the wedding
dress in the new collection. But for this it will be
necessary for you to cultivate a less sullen expression."

"Monsieur!" Lisette's sulky face cleared like magic.
"You say that *I* am to wear the wedding dress?"

"No, Lisette. I did not say that, and well you know
it," Florian assured her dryly. "Once more—no prom-
ises. What I said was that I *might* use you. A very different thing." Then, turning to Madame Moisant, he said,
"Madame, if I may have a word with you...." And the
two of them went out of the room.

Everyone now crowded around Lisette with an eagerness that made it plain to Loraine that the wearing of ·

the wedding dress in any new collection ranked as such an important favor that even the suggestion of being the fortunate one chosen conferred a special brilliance upon one.

She herself was left isolated near the door and, as Florian and his *directrice* paused outside, she distinctly heard Madame Moisant say, as though she could no longer suppress her protest, "Surely you would not really allow Lisette to wear the wedding dress?"

"No, of course not." The reply was cool, frank and brutal, though delivered in an undertone. "There is nothing bridal about Lisette. She is designed by nature for the Other Woman. It is the little Loraine who will make the perfect bride. She has all the qualities."

"You are already so sure?" Even Madame Moisant sounded a trifle incredulous.

"Of course. One does not have a flash of genius in stages," replied Florian without false modesty. "One knows."

"The other one will tear her to pieces," observed the *directrice* unemotionally.

"Between now and then she will learn to defend herself," was the careless reply.

Then they both went their separate ways, leaving Loraine divided between rapture and alarm. It seemed that her future path was to be fraught with most disagreeable perils. On the other hand, Florian had said she would probably wear the wedding dress. And already Loraine had absorbed enough of the dresshouse atmosphere to assess—and covet—this signal honor.

If one were to be torn to pieces by the dangerous Lisette, as Madame Moisant had so confidently prophesied, at least it would be in a splendid cause.

By the time the afternoon show began, Loraine was icy with fear and burning with enthusiasm. She was not aware that what she was experiencing was a form of stage fright. She only knew that, terrifyingly and miraculously, she was to play a part before strangers, and that her future with Florian's would depend on the way she played that part.

The other models, of course, had already shown these particular fashions so many times that they were without nerves and also without that first keen interest that spells adventure instead of routine. In contrast, Loraine was keyed up to the finest edge of competitive zeal. And perhaps this helped to highlight her performance.

At any rate, from the first moment she stepped out onto the small stage and moved forward along the raised platform in the little black suit—her heart thumping, her eyes starry and her lips faintly smiling—until the final retreat in her last number—a miracle of rose and lavender tulle that seemed to embody the dreams of every girl choosing her first evening dress—she was an unqualified success.

In some subtle exciting way, she knew it herself. She heard the murmur of it in the admiring indulgent comments of those who watched her. She saw the gleam of it in Florian's smiling but watchful eyes. And somewhere, deep down inside her, there was the inner conviction that this was her natural and inevitable form of self-expression. She was doing this thing well because it was as natural to her as breathing.

At the end, Madame Moisant said, "It was well done."

Clotilde said, "You were superb, *chérie*. Where were you trained?"

Lisette said, "She was amateur."

And Florian merely said, "Thank you, *mademoiselle*."

But she knew that those three words were her passport to the fashion world of Paris.

When the end of her first long long day came at last, Loraine felt both elated and exhausted. Never before had she gone through so many conflicting emotions in a matter of hours. And certainly never before had she so fully tasted the sweet heady wine of success.

She walked home through the shimmering evening

light, intoxicated with the beauty of Paris, the triumph of her happy achievement and the exquisite relief of having accepted a challenge and won. And when she finally came to the tall house that she now called home, she scorned the lift and rushed up the stairs to her guardian's apartment on the second floor.

The moment Mimi admitted her, she ran across the hall and into the drawing room, where Paul was lounging comfortably in an armchair, reading the evening paper.

"Hello!" He put down the paper and smiled across at her as she stood, pink cheeked and with shining eyes, in the doorway. "How did the first day go?"

"Wonderfully!" She came forward into the room as though she still walked on air. "I was a success."

"Already?" He looked amused but faintly indulgent, too. "How did you manage that?"

"It was like being in a book!" She pulled up a low stool and sat down in front of him, hugging her knees ecstatically like a little girl. She was so full of it all that she simply had to tell someone, and even her rather forbidding guardian seemed the ideal audience at the moment. "I didn't think I'd be allowed to show any dresses the very first day. But I was. Another girl, called Julie, had deser—I mean—" her voice dropped impressively "—she'd left Florian rather in the lurch by getting married and going to Australia."

"You appall me," murmured her guardian, and at that she laughed and leaned her arm upon his knee in an initmate little gesture that would have been utterly impossible twenty-four hours ago.

"It was so exciting—you can't imagine! Madame Moisant was doubtful if I should be allowed to show even one of Julie's dresses. But Florian tried me out in one outfit and then said, 'Let her have them all and see what she can make of them.' And Madame Moisant was quite shocked and said, 'All of them?' And he said, 'All of them—' just like that. Like—like—"

"An Eastern potentate ordering his harem about," suggested her guardian obligingly.

"Well, not quite like that. But with a sort of careless authority that was frightfully impressive."

"Don't lose your heart to Florian, dear child. He's very happily married," Paul reminded her.

"Oh, I *know* he is. And I'm not at all likely to lose my heart to him. It's just that he's so—so clever and unusual. But one wouldn't fall in love with him. He's quite old, isn't he?"

Her guardian made a face.

"About six years older than I am, I suppose."

"Oh," said Loraine, and looked reflectively at Paul, because she had really never thought about his age before.

"Well, anyway—" he seemed slightly anxious to break that scrutiny "—you then showed all the erring Julie's dresses very successfully?"

"Yes, indeed! It was quite a triumph."

"What did Florian say at the end?"

"He said, 'Thank you, *mademoiselle*,'" Loraine explained reverently, at which her guardian laughed insensitively and said that seemed meager praise in the circumstances.

"Oh, but it was the way he said it," Loraine assured him. "As though I'd done him a great favor and lifted a weight off his mind."

"Yes. They say Florian is very good at that sort of thing," agreed Paul, rubbing his chin thoughtfully. "But of course you had done him a favor and got him out of an awkward spot, if he really had lost one of his models in the middle of the season."

"Not the middle of it. Almost the end of it," said Loraine, who could not let that inaccuracy pass now that she was beginning to know her fashion world. "Everything is already beginning to lead up to the new collection, and everyone is mad with excitement and—" She pressed her hand against her lips and looked as though she had difficulty in holding back the next words.

"Come on—you'd better tell me the whole story." He smiled and looked amusedly curious.

"It's terribly secret, and I only overheard it, really. You will *keep* it secret, won't you?"

"I'll call on all my diplomatic training and do my best," he promised.

"Well, I overheard Florian say to Madame Moisant that he intended to have me model the wedding dress in the new collection."

"The wedding dress? But isn't that the high spot of the show?"

"Yes." She nodded vigorously. "That's why it's terribly exciting—and secret. Isn't it wonderful?"

"Wonderful," he agreed. "Can you bring yourself to eat some dinner now, do you think?"

"Oh, yes, please! I'm ravenous," Loraine declared. "I was too nervous to eat much at lunch. And anyway, there didn't seem to be much time."

"Well, don't let them starve you," said her guardian good-humoredly. "How did you get on with the other girls?"

"Very well. Except for one." Her face shadowed a little as she remembered the nasty brush with Lisette.

"You must tell me about her over dinner," Paul suggested.

And so, over their excellent dinner Loraine told him about Lisette's jealous outburst when Julie's dresses had been assigned to Loraine, after all. But she said nothing about the disagreeable way Lisette had catechized her with regard to the night of the opera gala. There was nothing she *could* tell her guardian about that.

The next day lacked the drama and thrills of the first day, of course. On the other hand, it was considerably less harrowing, and Loraine found herself quite naturally settling into the routine of the great dress house.

In the morning she was called on to display two of her models for a private customer, and as the afternoon hour approached for the beginning of the dress show, the now familiar tide of excitement began to rise within her.

She was not so nervous this time. After all, nothing like so much hung on this afternoon's performance. But even so, she stood trembling slightly with excitement and eagerness as she awaited her turn.

Lisette, indescribably provocative in a sea-green *tailleur*, drifted off the stage, and Clotilde stepped through the curtains to display the number that came before Loraine's black suit. And then, as Lisette passed, she said carelessly, "Your beau is out front there."

"My— What beau?" Loraine felt her throat tighten.

"The one who came in and kissed you at the opera."

"Philip!" exclaimed Loraine, and then could have bitten her tongue, for it was not part of her intention to give away the smallest bit of information about her affairs to Lisette.

"So he's Philip, is he?" Lisette smiled thoughtfully. "Yes, I remember now. I thought I'd seen him before. He's Philip Otway, the artist, isn't he?"

"Number Fourteen," hissed Madame Moisant warningly, and she shot an angry glance in Loraine's direction to let her know that she was not showing the proper degree of readiness.

Guiltily Loraine moved forward and, as Madame Moisant announced, "Number Fourteen"—this time in honeyed accents—she parted the curtains and stepped out onto the small stage.

Here she paused for a moment, as she had been instructed, before slowly and gracefully walking the length of the center platform. And as she did so, she saw that not only Philip, but Mrs. Otway, too, sat at the end of the room, smiling approvingly at her.

Loraine was not at all sure how much one was supposed to show that one was aware of anyone in the audience, so that the smile of recognition that she gave them was shy and brief. But because Philip was watching her, she walked indeed like a princess, and she told herself she had been right, hadn't she, when she had pretended that anything could happen when one wore the black suit.

Even when she turned and was on her way back, she knew that his smiling glance followed her, and she thought that no girl could ask for more than to appear before the man she loved in one Florian model after another. He could hardly think her a retiring schoolgirl now!

If the previous afternoon had been wildly exciting, this one was heartwarming, and Loraine enjoyed every moment of it. Toward the end of the show Florian came in, and she saw him speak to Mrs. Otway with the particular air that meant she was a well-liked customer.

She must have said something to him about knowing Loraine, for Florian smiled when Loraine next appeared and, as she turned at the end of the room, she heard him say, "Yes, she is very promising. You must have a word with her afterward."

Philip leaned forward then, and she thought she heard him say something about "more than a word." She dared not linger, but she returned to the dressing room fairly confident that he would find a way of arranging things the way he wanted them.

Sure enough, almost as soon as the show was over, Loraine was summoned back to the salon, now empty except for the Otways and Madame Moisant, who said with the graciousness she reserved for favored customers, "Here is the little Loraine, *madame. Petite*, you have visitors from England, it seems."

"Darling child!" Mrs. Otway, who was still a very beautiful woman indeed, enveloped Loraine in an expensively scented but genuinely tender embrace. "I simply couldn't believe it when Philip told me you were working here as a model."

"A very new one," Loraine said, smiling as she kissed Mrs. Otway and then turned to give her hand to Philip.

"We all have to be new once," observed Madame Moisant academically.

But Philip said immediately, "The amazing thing is that Loraine seems so completely professional and at ease."

"Monsieur Florian would not have taken her otherwise," Madame Moisant smiled thinly. "We have no room for the amateur here. Loraine will do very well if she works hard. And now, *madame*, which were the models that you wanted to see again?"

"The last two coats that Odette wore. And perhaps the one with the wide mink cuffs," replied Mrs. Otway promptly.

Then, as Madame Moisant went away to fetch Odette and the coats, she turned to her son and said, "If you've had enough of feminine clothes for one afternoon, Philip, we will excuse you."

"I'm afraid I have to go." He smiled down apologetically at Loraine, but in his handsome eyes there was a faintly puzzled look, as though, even now, he could not quite reconcile his recollections of a lonely schoolgirl with the apparently poised and lovely creature who seemed so much at home in Florian's salon.

"Oh, I'm sorry." She was as naively frank about that as if she were still a schoolgirl.

"So am I." He sounded genuinely regretful, too. "But let me take you to lunch tomorrow, Loraine."

"I'd love that! But it has to be rather a short one."

"Very well. I'll fetch you from here at—when?"

"A quarter to one?"

"Without fail," he promised. Then he bade his mother goodbye, just touched Loraine's smooth cheek with a caressing finger and went away.

Mrs. Otway looked after him. Then, as the silver gray curtains over the doorway fell to behind him, she said flatly and bitterly, "He's gone to meet that girl, of course."

"Oh." Loraine was so astounded at this unexpected reaction that for a moment she could only stare wordlessly at the older woman.

"A good deal has happened since we last saw each other, Loraine." Mrs. Otway shook her head impatiently. "Not only your father's death, you poor child. But

Philip's engagement, too. You do know he's engaged, of course?''

"He. . . mentioned it when I saw him at the opera," Loraine admitted diffidently. "Don't you. . . like her, Mrs. Otway?"

"No," said Philip's mother without elaboration.

"Does he know that's how you feel?"

"No, of course not. I should weaken my position immeasurably if I let him guess that. *She* knows, naturally. Women always sense these things. She's frigidly nice to me, of course, and I'm warmly nice to her because that's my way. But she knows that I don't mean that marriage to go through."

"Oh, Mrs. Otway!" Loraine tried to sound shocked and only succeeded in sounding excited. "But can you stop it?"

"I think so." Mrs. Otway's lovely face looked reflective and curiously ruthless. "I. . . think so. Particularly if you help me, Loraine. And you will, won't you? Because of course you love him, too, don't you?"

CHAPTER FOUR

UNTIL MRS. OTWAY said, "You love him, too, of course"—in a tone that implied a statement rather than a question—Loraine had hardly dared to admit to herself *how* much she loved Philip. But now it was almost as though the words conferred some sort of sanction on her secret feelings.

"How did you know?" She spoke in a low voice but she made no attempt to deny the fact.

"The way any intelligent mother knows, where her son is concerned." Mrs. Otway laughed indulgently. "In any case, it was almost inevitable. He played Prince Charming to you from the moment he discovered you. Even a much more experienced girl would have found him hard to resist."

"Oh," said Loraine, not altogether pleased by this reading of the case.

"Your reaction was very natural, darling." Mrs. Otway patted Loraine's cheek. "And, so far as I am concerned, very acceptable. Far more so than anything to do with this Elinor Roye he now wants to marry." And she pressed her lips together.

"But, Mrs. Otway, it *is* his own business whom he marries," Loraine pointed out reluctantly.

"Not entirely." Philip's mother sounded agreeable but emphatic. "Few men who are good-looking and susceptible—and Philip is both—succeed in finding themselves an ideal wife before some harpy snaps them up. That's where mothers are useful." She smiled a trifle complacently as she rearranged her sables. "When he telephoned me on Sunday morning—which he usually does—and mentioned that he had seen you, I seized the opportunity at once."

"The...opportunity?" Loraine said doubtfully.

"I was able to say, with perfect truth, that I had business here and that I would immediately combine it with a visit to make sure all was well with you. That, also, was perfectly sincere, you know, dear. I didn't quite like the idea of you all on your own in Paris, when you are young and...I suppose 'innocent' is the word."

Loraine laughed a little self-consciously.

"But I'm not really all on my own here. I—I have a guardian."

"Really? Philip didn't mention that." Mrs. Otway frowned, but as though she hardly thought a guardian improved matters.

"I didn't say much of him when I spoke to Philip. We had too little time to enlarge on anything."

"Him?" Mrs. Otway repeated the word reflectively. "The guardian is a man, then?"

"Yes. A—a sort of cousin of my father's," explained Loraine, once more resorting to this somewhat disingenuous way of describing Paul. For Mrs. Otway was too close to Philip—whatever her sympathies might be—for Loraine to dare risk giving her guardian's exact identity.

"A cousin of your father's? Some old man you hardly even knew, then?" Mrs. Otway spoke disparagingly. "Decidedly it was a good thing I came. Apart from the fact that I wanted to be here," she added with a mischievous smile. "And now—" she caught Loraine's hand with an air of flattering intimacy that was oddly disturbing "—we're in this together, aren't we?"

Loraine hardly knew what to say. It was, of course, quite wonderful to find that Philip's own mother thought it in his best interests that he should *not* marry this Elinor Roye. But the idea of being engaged in some sort of maternal conspiracy was most distasteful to her.

"I'm not sure what you think I—we could do." She

rather nervously returned the friendly pressure of the fingers holding hers. "Of course I want Philip to be happy and I wish he didn't feel his happiness was bound up with her. But one can't actually interfere, can one?"

"I can," stated Philip's mother calmly. "This girl merely filled a vacuum at a time when Philip was on his own and bored. What is required now is a powerful counterattraction. And that, dear Loraine, is you."

"*Me*, Mrs. Otway? Oh, but he thinks of me as a schoolgirl!"

"No, darling. That's how he did think of you. Now he is puzzled, charmed and intrigued to find you an amazingly attractive young woman. I was watching him each time the curtains parted and you appeared. And for minutes on end, I'll guarantee he forgot that Elinor Roye existed."

It was impossible to brush aside this dangerously attractive theory, and Loraine caught her breath on a half-guilty gasp of joy. Then, before she could think of anything to say either in protest or encouragement, Madame Moisant came hurrying back with apologies for her long absence, and Loraine was firmly sent back to her own duties, slightly dazed, slightly troubled but indescribably excited.

For the rest of the afternoon she was kept so busy that there was little time to think of her own affairs. And when she got home there was immediately something else to occupy her thoughts.

"I'm afraid I'm not going to be a very useful sort of guardian to you during the next three weeks, Loraine," Paul explained to her, half-apologetically. "I have to go to London on urgent business and I may have to fly on to Montreal from there. In other circumstances I might have taken you with me, I suppose. But since you're fixed up at Florian's, I imagine there's no question of that."

"None at all," Loraine assured him hastily, for nothing short of physical violence would have persuaded her to leave Paris after what Mrs. Otway had told her.

"Though it was kind of you even to think of taking me," she added hastily.

"Well, you *are* my concern, after all." Unexpectedly, he touched her dark hair with a not ungentle hand. "I feel rather badly about leaving you. But you're a good child, and I'm sure I can trust you not to get into any mischief while I'm away."

Illogically, this had the effect of making her want to blurt out the whole story about Philip and Elinor and Mrs. Otway's devious plans. But she firmly checked the confessional impulse and said instead that, under Mimi's care, she was certain she would do very well.

When she had time to think about it, her guardian's temporary absence from Paris did present some useful aspects. She would be free to see as much as she liked— or they liked—of both Philip and his mother during all that time, and she would be answerable to no one for the way she spent her evenings.

It was almost like a dispensation of Providence at this particular moment, Loraine thought gratefully. And, viewed in this light, Paul's departure in a couple of days' time seemed a legitimate reason for secret rejoicing, even if one felt a trifle guilty about it, too.

The next day, with her lunch appointment in view, Loraine dressed in the most becoming frock she possessed, and with such good result that Paul looked at her twice across the breakfast table and finally asked, "Does Florian reckon to dress all his models, even outside work hours?"

"I shouldn't think so! Why?" Loraine inquired in surprise.

"Well, that thing you're wearing now, for instance."

"*This?* This isn't a Florian model!"

"Isn't it?"

"Of course not! I bought it off the peg in London before I came here. Florian would have a fit if he thought anyone mistook it for one of his inspirations."

"I can bear the thought." Her guardian smiled slightly. "Perhaps it's the way you wear it."

"Oh, thank you. You mean I look nice?"

"I mean you look quite lovely," he assured her. "You're very happy about this Florian job, aren't you?"

"Very. But why do you ask?"

"You look so radiant this morning. Not at all like a girl who's going off to a routine job. More like someone who has some secret source of excitement and joy."

"Oh," said Loraine, and only by force did she prevent herself from blushing. "I—I suppose I do feel gay and on top of the world. But it's difficult not to in Paris, with the sun shining."

And then she bade him a hasty goodbye and departed for work.

On arrival, she was half scared, half flattered to be summoned almost immediately to Florian's workroom, where it seemed he was in a mood to design.

To Loraine it was a tiring but curiously exhilarating morning—her first experience of that combination of inspiration, concentration and frustration that would eventually result in something the fashion world would hail as a Florian creation.

He hardly spoke to her. She could have been a canvas-and-sawdust dummy for all the notice he took of her. And yet there was that strange intangible *rapprochement* between them that must exist between any creative artist and his source of inspiration.

As time wore on, she thought more than once of what Madame Moisant had said about aching heads and sagging arches. But only when she began to fear she might not be released in time for her appointment with Philip did she permit a small sigh to escape her.

He must have been more aware of her than he had shown, for he said, absently but not unkindly, "Not much longer, *petite*. Are you very tired?"

"No, *monsieur*." She straightened resolutely. "It wasn't that—" Then she checked herself quickly and hoped he was too much engrossed with his own affairs to have noticed what she had said.

A useless hope, indeed, as she realized the next moment.

"No? What then?" inquired Florian.

"Oh, it really doesn't matter." She was ashamed to have let her private considerations intrude upon the great man. But he merely waited and, after a moment, she explained humbly, "It's only that I—I have a lunch appointment."

"An important one?" he inquired as he flicked a length of shining silk around her and draped it with consummate skill, to fall in a cascade down the side of the skirt.

"To me—yes," Loraine confessed.

"Who is he?" The tone was faintly indulgent, though his attention seemed to be exclusively on the fall of the silk.

"*Monsieur!* I—I didn't say it was a *he*."

"At your age an important engagement is always with a *he*," Florian replied dryly. And, although she laughed, she found that she had to explain further.

"He is. . . an old friend, *monsieur*. Someone I knew at home in England. He happens to be in Paris—"

"The friend of whom you were thinking at Marianne's wedding?" inquired Florian, with a penetration that was all the more disconcerting because he still seemed to be giving only a fraction of his attention to Loraine and her affairs.

"*Monsieur*, h-how did you know?"

"By exercising my natural judgment, which is good, and a certain flair for inspired guesswork, which I possess," Florian told her without either conceit or false modesty.

Then he glanced at his watch and exclaimed, "It is already after half-past twelve. Come." He whipped the material off her with good-humored speed. "It is time you were off."

"Oh, *monsieur*! But your work isn't finished." In spite of Philip—and the flight of time—she was mortified at the idea that she might have proved unequal to the very first demand made upon her in the designing world.

"On the contrary, it is most satisfactorily finished."

"But—" she was more disappointed than she could have said "—there is no dress—no complete design."

He laughed.

"The design, *ma chère*, is here." He tapped his forehead. "And I assure you it is complete. I found what I wanted in the last three minutes. Go now and enjoy your lunch. What is his name, by the way?"

"His...name, *monsieur*? Philip," she admitted reluctantly, because there seemed no possible way of telling her employer to mind his own business.

"Philippe?" He repeated the name thoughtfully, giving it its French version. "Does your guardian know him?"

"My guardian?" she gasped. But this was really too much, and she found the courage to say, "Forgive me, *monsieur*, but—but is that your business?"

"I forgive you absolutely, *mon enfant*," replied the famous designer with a good deal of amusement. "My wife tells me I am inordinately inquisitive, though I call it taking an intelligent interest in my staff. However, perhaps she is right, so Monsieur Philippe shall be allowed to retain his aura of mystery. Now go. But on no account be late for this afternoon's show."

"Oh, no, *monsieur*," promised Loraine fervently, and she hurried away, faintly disturbed by the curious conviction that if Florian put himself out he could discover almost anything he wanted.

In spite of everything, she emerged from the dress house as the nearby church clock struck a quarter to one, and Philip waved to her from a car parked at the curb and exclaimed as she slipped in beside him, "Hello, sweet child! You're a model of punctuality."

"I very nearly wasn't," she told him with a breathless little laugh. "Florian was designing on me, and I was terrified he wouldn't finish in time."

"I should have waited, you know." Philip gave her a

smiling affectionate glance as he started the car. "It would have taken a lot to make me miss this meeting, Loraine."

Less than five minutes' driving brought them to a small quiet restaurant, where he had a corner table reserved and a swift attentive waiter to take care of their every want. Loraine relaxed with a sigh of contentment, impressed and charmed all over again that Philip always seemed able to make everything easy and enjoyable.

But once their meal was ordered, relaxation was at an end, for he smiled full at her and said, "Now tell me everything. I want the full story of the transformation of my little schoolgirl friend into a Paris model."

So, with an air of smiling candor that concealed a good deal of anxious thought, Loraine proceeded to give him a fairly comprehensive account of what had happened since her father's death.

It was not, of course, an impromptu effort. Ever since he had given the invitation the previous afternoon she had been working out, at intervals, what she should say to him when he asked the inevitable questions. And, without telling any actual untruth, she managed to lay much stress on the contact with Marianne and Roger Senloe, which had led to her engagement by Florian, while any reference to the guardian left him as a very shadowy and impersonal force in the background.

Then, as soon as she had brought Philip up-to-date with her affairs and before he could ask any awkward additional questions, she said, "And now it's your turn! I've done all the talking. You must tell me your news, too."

"I don't know that I have very much in comparison with your fantastic story." He smiled.

"Oh, Philip, of course you have! You told me at the opera. You're engaged, aren't you?"

"Well, yes. I'm engaged," he agreed, still smiling.

"Tell me about her," Loraine urged.

"She's fair and very lovely, and her name is Elinor Roye," he said obligingly.

"And when are you going to be. . . married, Philip?"

"We haven't really decided yet. We've been engaged only a matter of weeks, you know. We haven't been able to agree yet on where we shall live after we're married."

She wondered if that particular wording implied some degree of argument. But she said with an air of friendly interest, "Do you mean that you don't know whether to make it England or France?"

"Exactly. I'd like to live here in Paris—"

"Oh, Philip, would you?" She was half scared, half enchanted by the thought of him indefinitely in the same city as herself, whatever the future might hold.

"Yes. I find it artistically stimulating and professionally rewarding. In addition—" he laughed a little vexedly "—I don't need to tell you, Loraine, that I have a very charming, clever and altogether delightful mama—"

"Of course."

"But an incurably interfering one, too."

"Oh," said Loraine, and she felt a nervous little flutter in her throat that made it difficult to say more.

"To be frank, she doesn't really like the idea of my marrying at all," Philip went on. "The only thing that would have reconciled her to the idea would have been more or less to have chosen the girl herself. She's much too civilized and clever to *say* anything, of course, and we amiably avoid all argument. But if—when I start married life, it might be wiser to have the Channel between me and my charming parent, much as I love her."

"I see." Loraine tried to look deeply concerned and innocently unknowing at the same time. An almost impossible feat.

"You needn't look so solemn." He laughed lightly. "These things have a way of solving themselves."

"Yes, I suppose so. Have you explained the position to your fiancée?"

"Well, no, Loraine. No girl wants to be told that her future mother-in-law resents her and that it would be advisable to give her a wide berth for a while."

"Oh, no. And yet, for her part, she—your fiancée—" somehow Loraine could not bring herself to say Elinor's name "—prefers to live in England?"

"At least she is anxious not to settle in Paris."

"For any special reason?"

"Well, yes. The fact is, Loraine, that she was engaged to another fellow before she met me. He took the break extremely badly, and I think she would find it profoundly embarrassing if our two circles tended to cross."

"Perhaps," Loraine was astonished to hear herself say coldly, "she feels that she treated him rather badly."

"I don't think so." Philip sounded almost careless about that. "It was just a case of finding that she preferred someone else and having to tell him so."

"Regretfully?" inquired Loraine with quite unusual irony.

"Regretfully, I don't doubt." Philip still spoke as though they were discussing an unimportant aspect of the question. "These things are always difficult and upsetting."

"Particularly for the one who loses."

"Well, of course," Philip agreed with an easy laugh. "But I don't think you need shed any tears over Paul Cardine. He's a pretty tough nut."

"He's nothing of the sort! He's a very nice person," exclaimed Loraine indignantly, and then sat there staring at an astonished Philip, wondering what on earth had induced her to endanger her relationship with the man she really loved in order to fly to her guardian's defense in this inexplicable fashion.

"Why, Loraine...." Philip sounded amused, annoyed and wholly astounded. "You dark little horse! What do *you* know about Paul Cardine, for heaven's sake?"

"I've...met him more than once." She made a tremendous effort to retrieve the position. "And I like what I know of him. He was a friend of Roger Senloe's.

I met several people in their circle, you know, before
they married and went to Vienna.''

"And, of all people, there had to be Paul Cardine
among them!'' He gave a vexed little laugh.

"But we don't need to quarrel over that, do we,
Philip?'' she said anxiously.

"We're not going to quarrel over anything as far as
I'm concerned,'' he assured her.

"And it isn't necessary for us to. . . well, to enlarge on
the subject when I meet—if I meet—your fiancée?''

"Certainly not! And of course you'll be meeting
Elinor—and quite soon. We're going to see a lot of you
in the next few weeks. Which reminds me—'' he took
out a pocket diary and flicked over the pages ''—mother
suggested I should fix you up for dinner and a show
some time early next week. How about Monday? I'll
bring Elinor along and you can meet each other.''

Loraine said that would be lovely, and if she privately
excluded the meeting with Elinor from that general expression of approval, he was not to know.

When he parted from her again outside the Florian
boutique, he said, "It's wonderful having you around
again, little Loraine. We must do this often.''

And, if she had little time during the afternoon to
think in detail about her personal affairs, those last
remarks of his remained with her to warm and cheer a
somewhat anxious heart.

On the way home, however, as she walked through
the early-evening sunshine, she made a determined effort to review the rather tangled state of her personal
relationships.

At first she felt inclined to congratulate herself on the
way she had extricated herself from a very awkward
situation with Philip. It had been ridiculous of her to
rush to Paul's defense like that, inevitably disclosing the
one connection it was vital to hide. But at least she had
retrieved the position well. Or so it seemed to her.

But then as she looked farther ahead, she had to admit that she had put herself in a very false position. It

was one thing to make little of her guardian's part in her life. It was quite another to suppress the fact that he was the very man Philip was talking about. Particularly as Philip must inevitably find out the deception eventually.

That was the really disturbing fact. However ingenious she might be, and however long she might hold off discovery of the real position, the time must eventually come when, unless he passed out of her life altogether, she occupied such an important place that he must know her home circumstances.

But anything may have happened by then, Loraine assured herself. *It's all a matter of timing. For him to know the real position now would drive a wedge of embarrassment and distrust between us. But if he and Elinor do not get married after all, and if he then turns to me instead, he won't care whether I'm Paul's ward or not. Still less will he mind that I concealed that embarrassing fact for the time being.*

There were some powerful "ifs" about this line of reasoning, she knew. But, like most of us when we see a distant but infinitely desirable goal, she found little difficulty in gliding over the provisos and arriving at the satisfactory conclusion.

When she reached home she found that her guardian had decided to give her an enjoyable last evening before his departure, and he took her for the promised dinner at Maxim's.

Loraine's knowledge of Paris life was rapidly expanding, but it had not so far included anything like this, and she gazed around, wide-eyed, in a way that seemed both to please and amuse her guardian.

"Why do you watch me in that amused way?" she asked once as she caught his slightly smiling glance at her across the table.

"I don't know, Loraine—except that you're a pleasure to watch, I suppose. And one doesn't often have the experience of taking out anyone with your enormous capacity for enjoyment."

"Oh—" she frowned slightly "—you mean I'm frightfully young and naive, I suppose?"

"You're not frightfully anything," he informed her dryly.

"But I'm not—" she glanced around and made a vague comprehensive gesture "—elegant and sophisticated and poised, like most of the women here. I wish I were! It must be marvelous to look and feel as though you can deal with any situation."

"But for that, my dear, you would have to give up your priceless gift of youth."

"Oh, that!" she said, and she actually pouted slightly, for at the moment she felt a trifle too young.

"And possibly the even more priceless gift I mentioned before. Your incredible capacity for enjoying yourself."

"Is that so important?" She looked at him curiously.

"I'd say it's the basis of your particular charm, Loraine," he told her, so seriously that she had the strange impression he had been studying her a good deal during the weeks she had lived in his apartment. "Perhaps it's the chief ingredient in almost any charm," he added reflectively. "There's something so warm and radiant about enjoyment, and so chilling and sterile about boredom or even humdrum acceptance. I never thought much about it before, but since you came the charm of sheer enjoyment has been quite a discovery for me."

She was so touched and surprised that she could only stare at him for a moment. And then, as she did so, she saw his expression change and harden as his glance came to rest on someone who was evidently approaching their table from behind her.

Even before she saw him incline his head in a cold little gesture of greeting, Loraine guessed who it was, and in sudden panic she lowered her head and pretended to be absorbed in her meal.

By the time she dared to look up again, Elinor Roye had passed and, with a sense of relief that almost hurt, Loraine saw that her companion was not Philip. As far as she could judge from the back view, she thought it was the elegant elderly lady to whom Elinor had been speaking on the night of the opera gala.

They went to a distant table, where Elinor sat with her back to the room, and slowly Loraine's gaze returned to her guardian. There had been such a long pause that she simply had to say something and what she said was, "Who was that?"

"Someone I know."

"Do you know her well?"

"I used to think so, Loraine." He gave a short laugh. "But now I'm not so sure. We were engaged until a few weeks ago."

"Oh, I'm terribly sorry. That was the personal crisis you said happened just about the time I arrived?"

"Yes."

"Were you dreadfully unhappy about it, Paul?"

"No man likes to be jilted," he said dryly.

"No, of course not. It's an affront to one's pride as well as one's affections. But there are degrees of being miserable, aren't there? I mean, hurt pride is something one gets over fairly soon, I imagine. Whereas crushed feelings take a lot longer."

To her surprise he laughed quite heartily at that.

"A very wholesome and Loraine-like analysis," he declared mockingly. "But then you're not proud, are you?"

"No, I don't think so. At least, not in a puffed-up, biblical way. I was glowing with pride when Florian said I would make a good model, and I'm not going to pretend I don't like the idea—" she dropped her tone to a discreet whisper "—of wearing the wedding dress in the new collection. But that's all."

"And suppose—" he studied her smilingly "—one of the others got the wedding dress after all?"

"Oh, I'd *hate* that," admitted Loraine promptly, at which he laughed more than she had ever seen him laugh before and declared that he was glad to see that she was charmingly human.

Although they lingered enjoyably over their meal, they left the restaurant before there was any question of Elinor and her companion coming their way again, for which Loraine was profoundly thankful. If, as Philip had arranged, they were to meet each other on the following Monday evening, it was vital that she should not be registered on Elinor's memory as the girl who had been dining at Maxim's with Paul Cardine.

Next morning the goodbyes were said. She thought perhaps her guardian might kiss her, in view of their improved relations. But evidently the idea did not occur to him.

He simply said, "I'll drop you a line to let you know if I have to go on to Montreal. Otherwise, enjoy yourself. And if any crisis arises, which I don't anticipate, you'd better consult Florian. He can deal with most things."

"Consult Florian?" Loraine was quite scandalized at the idea. "I don't imagine he expects to be troubled with our unimportant private affairs. I wouldn't dream of speaking to him about a personal problem."

"On the contrary," her guardian replied coolly. "He was rather flattered when I telephoned him, explained the position and asked him to see you came to no harm."

"You did that?" She was both shocked and intrigued. "When?"

"Just after you left here yesterday morning."

"What on earth did he say?"

"His exact wording was 'I am gratified, *monsieur*, that you should think me suitable for the task.' Which was, of course, his rather Gallic way of saying, 'Certainly, old chap. Depend on me,'" replied Paul, and his eyes twinkled unexpectedly.

Loraine laughed, but reluctantly, and her guardian asked mildly, "Do you object to the arrangement?"

"No, of course not!" She was anxious that he should have no inkling that she had been rejoicing in the thought of no supervision. "Only...Florian's a bit interfering by nature, and a French guardian is a very different proposition from an English one.''

"He hasn't had all my guardianly duties delegated to him," Paul assured her. "But he will be available if you need advice or support at any time."

"Well, thank you. It was kind of you to think of it," Loraine said. Then she bade him a hasty goodbye, since it was getting late, and set off to work in a somewhat divided state of mind.

It was reassuring, of course, to know that in the unlikely event of a real crisis the worldly and resourceful Florian was there. On the other hand, she remembered with some disquiet those casual questions about Philip—and with even more disquiet his almost genial remark that he took an intelligent interest in the affairs of his staff.

CHAPTER FIVE

DURING THE NEXT FEW DAYS, Loraine's life began to settle into the most enjoyable routine. Mimi was an admirable housekeeper, so that Loraine had no domestic cares at all. And few are the people who could not be satisfied with a flat in Paris in those circumstances, allied to a fascinating job in one of the great dress houses.

At work the whole tempo was quickening daily—Loraine sometimes thought hourly—and the first faint wind of change and challenge was beginning to blow through the place. Now no one talked of anything but the new collection, and although jealousies, slights and crises, tearful or otherwise, were still very much part of life in the models' dressing room, there was also a sort of corporate loyalty that bound them all together in the great enterprise of staking the claim of *their* dress house against all others in the ever recurring battle for success.

It was impossible to remain immune from the fever of ambition and determination. And like all the others, Loraine found herself ready to put aside weariness—or, indeed, almost any other personal consideration—if she could thus contribute in the smallest degree to the brilliance of The Day.

All the same, Monday evening shone brightly in prospect, and she ran out eagerly enough when Philip appeared, as arranged, to collect her.

"I'm taking you to mother's hotel first," he explained, "and leaving you there while I go for Elinor. Then we'll all dine there and go on afterward to this new Russian variety show that everyone seems to think is so marvelous."

"It sounds a lovely arrangement," Loraine said. And, indeed, it did meet with her approval, for she was glad to have the opportunity of a few words with Mrs. Otway before the more general meeting took place.

At the hotel—one of the most expensive and exclusive in Paris, Loraine noted, because she was beginning to understand about these things—she discovered that Mrs. Otway had a very pleasant suite. Evidently it was not part of her plan to do herself anything but well while in the process of overseeing her son's matrimonial affairs.

"Come and sit down, darling. I suppose you're exhausted with standing all day. But how pretty you look, just the same." Mrs. Otway smiled approvingly at Loraine, in a charming way that had the subtle and altogether acceptable effect of making her feel her best. "I never realized the child was going to grow into such a beauty. Did you, Phil?"

"I always thought her a beauty," was his calm reply. "But now she is a more self-possessed beauty with a delightful touch of the unexpected about her. Have fun gossiping, you two. I'll be back in less than half an hour."

"That's just what we mean to have, isn't it, dear?" Mrs. Otway declared mischievously as the door closed behind him. "How did the luncheon date go?"

Immediately Loraine felt that faintly uncomfortable sensation that Mrs. Otway's conspiratorial air had induced in her before.

"It was lovely." She tried to sound extremely matter-of-fact but was afraid she only succeeded in sounding slightly secretive. "Quite short, of course. But at least we had time to catch up on each other's news. I think Philip was a good deal amused to hear about my Florian job."

"And, in return, told you all about his engagement?"

"Among other things—yes. Not *all* about it. He just told me the bare fact and described her."

But Mrs. Otway was not at all prepared to let it go at

that. Like a good general reviewing the various aspects of a campaign, she said pleasantly, "Philip tells me that you actually know Elinor's first fiancé. Such a coincidence!"

"Ye-es. At any rate, I've met him." Once again instinct told her that she must not confide to any degree in this charming inquisitive woman.

"And you like him, according to Philip."

"I do like what I've seen of Paul Cardine and I said so quite frankly. I'm afraid I rather gave Philip the impression that I was taking sides, in some way. Of course I wasn't. It was just that I know Paul and I don't know her. I suppose I naturally tended to sound as though my sympathies were with him."

"You don't need to apologize, my dear. You know where *my* sympathies lie." And Mrs. Otway gave a wry little smile. "I expect she treated the poor man pretty badly. She's rather a ruthless young woman, as you will see for yourself."

"Oh, please! I'd much rather not talk about her beforehand," Loraine said uncomfortably. "It will make me feel dreadfully self-conscious when she arrives. Can't we talk about something else?"

"If that's how you feel." The older woman seemed amused rather than offended—possibly because she felt she had already found out all she wanted to know. "How are all the plans for the new collection going?"

"Oh, wonderfully, I'm sure." Loraine turned to the fresh subject with relief. "Not, of course, that I have anything but a very scrappy knowledge of things. But the general drive and excitement is quite thrilling. And Monsieur Florian himself looks so coolly confident that we all feel everything will be fine."

"I expect he has his frantic moments, all the same," Mrs. Otway said a little callously.

"After all these years of success?" Loraine looked doubtful.

"All the more because of his years of success." Mrs. Otway gave a knowledgeable little shake of her head.

"When you've clawed your way to the top, the really harrowing test is to stay there. Imagine a Florian show that was *not* a success."

"Oh, I couldn't!" Loraine turned quite pale at the thought. "Particularly the very first one I was in. I can't tell you how much I want it to be a triumph for him."

"Yes? They say he inspires all his staff with that almost fanatical loyalty." Mrs. Otway gave her an amused considering glance. "Well, darling, I shall certainly be there on the first day to cheer you on."

"Thank you."

"But that reminds me—I don't imagine telephone calls will be very popular at the salon during the coming weeks. You'd better give me your home number, dear child, so that I can get in touch with you more easily."

For a moment Loraine experienced one of those moments of panic that were the penalty of trying to keep one half of her life divorced from the other. Then her common sense told her that Paul's telephone number could have no significance for Mrs. Otway, and it was in the remotest degree improbable that she would have occasion to discuss it with Elinor, of all people.

So with an air of great candor, she said, "It's Palais Four-Three-Three-Two," and congratulated herself on the fact that this inquiry had so fortunately been made before Elinor herself came on the scene.

"I'll write it down now," Mrs. Otway declared, and she proceeded to do so in a very elegant little white-and-gold kid notebook that she returned to her handbag—to Loraine's relief—just as the door opened to admit Philip and Elinor Roye.

It was not an easy encounter for Loraine. It could not have been in any circumstances. For she might entertain what hopes she liked—even give reluctant ear to Mrs. Otway's wishful thinking—but the fact remained that this was the girl Philip had asked to marry him.

In addition, Elinor Roye was not a girl who made other girls feel their best. She was almost disconcertingly lovely and well groomed, with a cool beauty that made other noses feel shiny and other hair untidy. Her smile was charming and her voice exceedingly well pitched. But these qualities somehow combined to give an air of graciousness, and although graciousness exalts the dispenser, it frequently abashes the recipient.

From the moment Elinor smiled calmly and said, "How do you do?" with full value on each syllable, Loraine felt two inches shorter and three years younger than she had before.

Mrs. Otway, of course, managed everything beautifully and contrived to give the general impression that this was the meeting she had been longing for for years. But although throughout dinner she sought to stimulate Loraine to great liveliness and what she would undoubtedly have characterized as intelligent competition, Loraine instinctively withdrew more and more into herself and became very much the shy young friend from the undistinguished past.

She must, she feared, have been a considerable disappointment to Mrs. Otway.

Things were somewhat easier once they arrived at the theater, for at least there was no need for scintillating conversation except during the intervals. But just as Loraine was beginning to recover her poise a little she made the agitating discovery that Florian and his wife were sitting not far away.

Nothing, of course, could have been more correct and proper than the family party in which she found herself. But all the same, Loraine could not help feeling a certain degree of self-consciousness when, in the second interval, her employer stood up, glanced carelessly around the theater and immediately noticed her.

He bowed politely to her and Mrs. Otway. Then his glance traveled on speculatively for a moment to rest on Philip and Elinor. She *knew* Philip could be no more than "Mr. Otway" to him. They had probably exchanged no more than a dozen words when he accompanied his mother to the salon. And yet—as though Philip had his name embroidered on his shirtfront—she saw the knowledge leap into her employer's mind that here was the man with whom she had had the important lunch date.

Fortunately there was no attempt at conversation between the two parties during this interval or the next. But as they were slowly making their way out of the theater at the end of the performance, Loraine was not very much surprised to find Florian at her elbow.

"Did you enjoy yourself, *petite*?" he inquired quite kindly.

"Very much, thank you. Did you?" She had become a little separated from the others and that helped her to be more at ease.

"As much as I ever enjoy anything when I have the collection on my mind," Florian said with a slight grimace.

"Oh, I'm sorry!"

"You don't need to be. One must pay some sort of price for success," the great designer conceded frankly. "And Monsieur Philippe—did he enjoy himself?"

She was exasperated but she was also reluctantly amused by his tactics.

"I think so."

"The lady who completed your party is very charming."

"Mrs. Otway, do you mean?" said Loraine, thinking that he deserved that.

"No." He pinched her ear sharply. "The other one. Who is she?"

She thought of saying it was her maiden aunt. But then she decided that one must not take too many liberties with Florian, even when he was in a good mood.

So she said a trifle sulkily, "Monsieur Philippe's fiancée. And I shouldn't be surprised if she comes to the opening day with Mrs. Otway in order to choose some of her trousseau."

"Ah," said her employer reflectively, "then we must try to find something to please her. But not the wedding dress, I think. That will express a very different personality."

Then he bade Loraine good-night and went away, leaving her curiously excited about the wedding dress, and the way it would express the personality of the one who wore it.

As she rejoined her own party, Mrs. Otway was just saying that it would be too dull to go straight home—that, in fact (and how right she was!), half the fun of going to a good show is to sit and discuss it afterward in congenial company.

"All Continental café life is built around that excellent principle," she declared. "And the fact that British catering persistently ignores it accounts for the dreariness of half the cities in England."

So, in vindication of her views, they all went on to a gay and charming restaurant, and Loraine began to feel her confidence and natural good spirits returning. Whether it was what Florian had said about the wedding dress or not, she could not have said, but she suddenly found herself able to smile and talk and hold her own, even when Elinor's coolly reflective glance rested on her—as it did once or twice—for an embarrassing length of time.

It was Philip who finally said, "We mustn't forget that our Loraine is a working girl, mother. It's time she was home and in bed."

And not until that moment did Loraine realize that the process of depositing her at home involved a considerable degree of risk—even disaster—if Elinor should accompany her and see where she was living.

For a second she felt blank. Then with an air of decision that Elinor herself could not have improved upon, she said, "You take Elinor home, Philip. Your mother and I will have a taxi. I can drop her off at her hotel and go on."

"Or I can drop you off, dear." The faint edge in Mrs. Otway's usually pleasant speaking voice was the only sign of her extreme annoyance at being forestalled on the question of homegoing arrangements. "Or why don't we—"

"We can settle that in the taxi." Loraine smiled, but with a pleasant firmness there was no gainsaying. "And now I really *must* go. I had no idea it was so late."

The party broke up while Philip was still saying something about being perfectly able to take everyone home. But Loraine patted his arm in something commendably like a sisterly way and said, "Don't be silly. You and Elinor want *some* time alone together, I'm sure."

A remark that Mrs. Otway evidently considered so foolishly uncooperative that she could hardly conceal her irritation. With an effort, however, she produced her sweetest smile and declared firmly that they must see dear Loraine again very soon.

"Yes, indeed!" In spite of Elinor's presence, Philip did not conceal his eagerness about that. "I'll phone you at Florian's."

"Better make it her home address," suggested his mother. "Telephone calls will be taboo at Florian's during the next few weeks, I imagine."

"Of course." He turned to Loraine. "What's the number?"

"I have it." And before Loraine could invent a new number or resort to any other desperate remedy, Mrs. Otway opened her bag and produced the white-and-gold notebook. "It's—" she flicked over the pages "—Palais Four-Three-Three-Two."

"Palais Four-Three-Three-Two," repeated Philip, scribbling it down on the back of the restaurant bill.

"Palais Four-Three-Three-Two?" repeated Elinor softly, but on a rising note of query. Her eyes met Loraine's widened frightened ones. Then she just dropped her glance and murmured, "How...odd." But so quietly that only Loraine heard.

"The taxi is here, *monsieur*," said the waiter, coming up at that moment. And never, it seemed to Loraine, had sweeter, more intelligent words been uttered.

By hurrying through the good-nights at top speed she contrived to avoid Elinor's speculative glance again, and at last she was safely in the taxi with Mrs. Otway, though so limp with suppressed nervousness that presently her companion said, "How quiet you are, darling. I hope it wasn't in some way a disappointing evening for you."

"No, of course not!" Loraine roused herself determinedly. "It was a perfectly lovely evening. The show was just as good as the report said and—"

"Oh, the *show*." Mrs. Otway did not seem to consider that of much importance in the evening's program. "I was thinking of more personal things." Then she added with the faintest touch of asperity, "If you had left the homegoing arrangements to me, Loraine, it would have been better. I intended Elinor to share my taxi and Philip to take you home."

"I think the other way worked very well," replied Loraine.

Mrs. Otway seemed to find this too silly and inexplicable to be even worthy of comment, so they lapsed into silence. And only when the taxi began to slow down outside the handsome house in which Paul Cardine had his apartment did she lean forward with interest and say, "So this is where you live, Loraine? A very pleasant situation."

"It's very convenient for my work," Loraine explained, as though that were her sole reason for living in one of the most distinguished parts of the city. "I'm able to walk there and back."

"Very nice," commented her companion. But she glanced at Loraine as though it struck her for the first time that perhaps she was not handling quite such simple material as she had supposed.

However, she kissed Loraine very kindly, bade her good-night and watched from the taxi until she was safely inside the doorway—an attention that Loraine appreciated, even though the unworthy thought passed through her mind that Mrs. Otway was possibly just making quite sure that she did live there.

"I'm just thinking nasty things because I'm so scared about what has happened," Loraine told herself as she fumbled for her key and quietly let herself into the flat.

Mimi would have gone to bed long ago, she knew, and it was a completely deserted place into which she stepped. But even so, in some inexplicable way, the atmosphere of her guardian's home closed around her with a suggestion of reassurance and comfort.

It was partly the contrast of warmth, after coming in out of the cool night air, she supposed. But it was also the subtle feeling that here, in some indefinable sense, she belonged and was safe.

But when she reached her room she could not immediately go to bed. She walked about softly, talking to herself under her breath in a stream of agitated question and answer.

"What will Elinor do about it? Will she have told Philip even now, on the way home, that my telephone number is inexplicably the same as Paul's? And what will Philip think? Oh, why didn't I tell him the truth from the very beginning? It would have been so much simpler really. Except that he might have decided regretfully to see no more of me. Only now, if she wants to make trouble, I've simply handed her the ammunition on a plate."

At this hour, and in her present state of mind, it did not even strike Loraine as an odd way to pass ammunition. She could only think about Elinor and the damage she could do or not do, as she chose.

And yet, if Elinor did want to make trouble, why had she not said something right away—there in the restaurant? Loraine's discomfiture would have been complete.

Was it—and here, for a moment, the first gleam of hope entered the argument—was it perhaps that she was no more anxious than Loraine to have Paul brought into the conversation? After all, he could hardly be a comfortable topic as far as she and her fiancé were concerned. And certainly not with Mrs. Otway standing by.

Loraine sat down on the side of her bed and, for the first time since her telephone number had been mentioned, she felt her tense nerves relax. Whatever Elinor had thought—and surely even she must have felt some sort of curiosity, if nothing else—she had deliberately chosen to say nothing. That in itself was hopeful.

It was not, of course, possible to feel entirely reassured. But at last Loraine felt sufficiently calmed to go to bed and, since she was young and healthy, almost immediately to sleep.

The next morning much of her anxiety returned at the moment of waking. But she then discovered that she had overslept, and over a hurried breakfast and a rush to work she had no time to indulge in anxious reflection.

The day, like so many days now, was spent almost entirely in designing and fitting. And although part of the time she felt she could willingly drop on the ground and stay there, she was also sustained by the proud and exhilarating thought that all this meant she was an element—possibly a vital element—in the magical concern, the new Florian collection.

She had so successfully thrust her own affairs to the back of her mind that her heart gave an uncomfortable skip or two when, at the end of the afternoon, Florian said gravely, "Sit down, *mademoiselle*. I have something to say to you."

He seldom called her *mademoiselle*, and she thought at first that he was going to reprimand her for something. But almost immediately she realized that he was merely impressing her with the importance of the occasion.

He leaned back against his desk, his arms folded, and regarded her with those uncomfortably penetrating gray eyes.

"You have seen enough now," he told her, "to realize that twice a year every great dress house goes on fresh trial before a pretty pitiless audience. None of us is exempt. And to every one of us the most important weapon in the contest is the element of surprise. That is why, if secrets leak out before their time, the whole show can be a failure. You understand this?"

"Yes, *monsieur*." She was deeply impressed and her tone showed it.

"Good. Now, as with a book or a play, a dress show requires a dramatic opening and a heart-catching close. In certain circumstances it can survive a tame opening, though this is dangerous. But no dress show has ever survived a finale that is either tame or lacking in the element of surprise. This, then, throws upon the Wedding Dress—" his tone conferred capital letters upon it "—and on the one who wears it, the heaviest responsibility in the whole show."

He paused again, and she said, "Yes, *monsieur*," in a subdued whisper.

"I have decided, *mademoiselle*, to let you wear the wedding dress in the new collection," Florian stated with telling simplicity. And so effective was his way of making the announcement that, although Loraine had entertained hopes of this ever since she had overheard his words to Madame Moisant, the confirmation of her hopes actually brought tears into her eyes—a tribute that Florian obviously both marked and approved.

"*Monsieur*, I—I'm overwhelmed. I...don't know what to say," Loraine gasped at last.

"Then say nothing," Florian advised her dryly. "For that is what you are going to have to contrive to do, in the strictest sense, during the next two or three weeks. First, I want you to say nothing about my choice to the other girls until I choose to make the matter known myself. There will be enough trouble then— as always," he added sardonically. "Then to no one— to absolutely no one, you understand—must you disclose one single detail of the dress itself."

"Oh, Monsieur Florian, I wouldn't dream of it!"

"Oh, yes, you would—just like everyone else," he assured her. "After a while you will become so obsessed with the secrecy of it all that this is exactly what you *will* do—dream of it. And then you will wake, sweating with terror lest you have been talking in your sleep. At least, I hope you will," he added callously.

"For this will show that you have the right attitude of mind."

"*Monsieur*, I promise you that not the smallest hint shall escape me," Loraine declared earnestly, and only with difficulty did she keep herself from crossing her heart, so impressive did the occasion seem.

"*Bon!*" He smiled at her, suddenly and brilliantly. "And, in return, *I* will promise *you* that every man— but every one—who attends the opening show will see in you the perfect, the inevitable bride."

"Oh!" She laughed and colored. "That could be rather embarrassing, though, couldn't it?"

"Not," Florian assured her dryly, "if you keep your head. See only that Monsieur Philippe accompanies his admirable *maman* on this occasion."

"Oh!" she said again, and this time she went scarlet, for she suddenly realized what Florian meant. "But— but, Monsieur Florian, his fiancée will be coming, too."

"Yes, I remember. You told me as much. And, as I told you, we will try to find something to please her. But not the wedding dress, *chérie*. Not the wedding dress."

And, on that, Florian smilingly dismissed her.

Loraine walked home in a mood of jubilation. Of faintly guilty jubilation perhaps, for she kept on re- minding herself that it was both mean and paltry to have designs—even in thought—on another girl's fiancé.

But then it was not as though she were called on to take any sort of action, one way or the other. All she had to do was to wear the Florian wedding dress—in all probability the wedding dress of the year—and if the results were in- deed as sensational as Florian had prophesied, what possible reason would she have to reproach herself?

True, she was by no means out of the woods with regard to the telephone incident the previous evening. A cloud fell on her spirits when she recalled this, and reluctantly she faced the fact that Philip might, even now, be thinking of her as a secretive, oddly deceitful young person who had inexplicably withheld a tricky piece of personal information.

She felt scared all over again at that thought. But the interview with Florian must have bolstered her morale even more than she had realized. For, when she reached home, she suddenly decided that, rather than wait for the blow to fall, she would boldly telephone Philip herself and judge from his attitude whether or not Elinor had chosen to say anything.

No sooner had she dialed his number than her courage deserted her, and she would have replaced the receiver if Philip's voice had not almost immediately sounded in her ear.

"Hello, it's Loraine," she said on a little gasp of mingled fright and excitement.

"Loraine, dear! How nice to hear from you. Are you at Florian's?"

"No, I'm at home." She actually gulped in her relief, for—there was no doubt of it—his interest was as affectionate and undisturbed as ever. "I just wanted to ring and thank you once more for a perfectly lovely evening."

"It was lovely for me, too," he assured her. "We must do it again, my dear. Don't let Florian work you so hard that there's no time to play."

"I won't." She laughed gaily, although, of course, there was not the slightest prospect of her affecting Florian's plan of work one way or the other, and they knew it. "Give my love to your mother, won't you?"

"Of course. And keep some evenings free for me— for us. How are you fixed for next weekend?"

"There's nothing at the moment."

"Then we'll arrange something," he declared. "I'll call you up in a day or two, dear."

And then he bade her goodbye, and Loraine, glowing with happiness and breathless with relief, replaced the receiver. Either Elinor had, for her own reasons, said nothing to him about that curious business of the telephone number. Or else—even pleasanter possibility—he attached no importance to it in any case.

She sat there for a minute or two longer, lost in pleasant reflection. Then, just as she rose to go and get ready for dinner, the telephone bell rang again.

Immediately there flashed into her mind the delightful possibility that it was Philip ringing with some new and enchanting suggestion, and she leaned forward and snatched up the receiver once more.

But it was not Philip's warm friendly voice that sounded in her ear. It was Elinor's cool, well-pitched tones, which said, "Is that Loraine Darnell?"

Loraine was tempted to say it was not and replace the receiver. But she knew instinctively that Elinor had already recognized her when she said, "Hello." So, although her heart began to beat heavily, she replied as brightly as she could, "Why, yes. Is that Elinor?"

"It is." Very slight pause. Then: "I expect you know why I'm contacting you."

"N-no. Is it something special?"

"It may not be my business. But I should very much like to know why you're living in Paul Cardine's apartment," Elinor's voice stated calmly and categorically.

"Oh!" Something in the wording made Loraine feel so indignant that she blurted out the truth immediately. "He's my guardian."

"*Paul* is?" For a moment even Elinor seemed put off her stroke. "But why doesn't anyone know about it? Philip hasn't the faintest idea, has he?"

"No!" In spite of all her efforts, that sounded sharp and anxious. "I thought it would be more...comfortable all round if I didn't enlarge on the position."

"But you must have gone to quite a lot of invention and deceit to keep the fact hidden. It hardly seems worthwhile."

"I thought it was," Loraine stated, more calmly now because she was beginning to recover herself.

"Yes, I see you might," was the thoughtful reply, and immediately Loraine felt terribly anxious again because of the odd note in the other girl's voice.

Once more there was a slight pause. Then Elinor said, deliberately and distinctly, "I don't believe in a lot of plain speaking, usually. But there are occasions when it's essential, and I think this is one of them. You're very keen to marry Philip yourself, aren't you? No, don't bother to answer. I know simply by watching you. And of course his mother is on your side because she knows she can manage you, whereas I would stand no nonsense—''

"Please don't say such things! It isn't as though—"

"Just a moment. Let me finish. You didn't tell Philip you were Paul's ward because it would have made meetings very difficult, perhaps impossible. I don't blame you. I'd have done the same in your place. But I'm not in your place, Loraine, and I'm looking after *my* side of things. I have enough stacked against me with Mrs. Otway to handle. I don't intend to have you around, too. Make what excuses and explanations you like but keep out of Philip's way for the time being."

"Keep out of Philip's way? How dare you say anything so—so silly and impertinent to me!" exclaimed Loraine indignantly.

"Because I hold the trump card," was the cool and literal reply, made in such a matter-of-fact tone that it carried complete conviction. "You'd better be so busy at Florian's during the coming weeks that you have no time or energy for seeing people. Or else. . . ."

"Or else what?" Loraine was fascinated into asking.

"Or else I shall explain to Philip that I find you're living in Paul Cardine's flat, in circumstances you're anxious to keep hidden from your closest friends," replied Elinor.

Then the line went dead, and Loraine was left staring in front of her, the silent receiver still in her hand.

CHAPTER SIX

FOR A WHOLE MINUTE Loraine remained absolutely still. Then she slowly replaced the receiver and said out loud, "But that's ridiculous! My position here is perfectly clear and straightforward. She knows it. And she knows it would be simple enough to explain that fact to Philip. At least...."

Loraine passed her hands over her face and smoothed back her hair in sudden fresh perplexity.

It was true there was little question of any actual damage to her reputation. Elinor knew, as well as she did, that the unpleasant way of putting things merely served to highlight the peculiar secrecy of her behavior. But once the subject had been broached—and broached in that startling and distasteful manner—Philip would be in no mood to take an indulgent view of her extraordinary lack of candor.

Her whole conduct in concealing the position would appear questionable, just when she most wanted to stand well with him. And Philip might even—prompted by Elinor—take the view that her curious behavior was all part of some joint scheming with his mother.

Her cheeks began to burn at the very thought of trying to explain things to him, in the certain knowledge that Elinor intended to put her in as bad a light as possible. Unless, that was, Loraine accepted her terms and merely kept out of the picture for the time being.

To do so would, she knew, be little better than yielding to moral blackmail. And, somehow, the fact that Elinor appeared so cool and civilized made these tooth-and-claw methods seem all the more shocking.

On the other hand, deep down inside her, Loraine felt

a curious pang of reluctant sympathy for her adversary. As Elinor had said with devastating candor, she had enough to contend with in Mrs. Otway without having Loraine to confuse the issue. And, for good or ill— whether one liked it or not—she *was* the girl Philip had asked to be his wife, and that did entitle her to some sort of prior rights.

One might justify one's inmost hopes with the specious arguments that Elinor had been ruthless over her engagement, that she would not really make Philip happy, even that his own mother thought the whole thing a mistake. But one could not justify any active interference.

I wasn't really going to attempt that anyway, Loraine thought defensively. *But then she was not to know that. She probably thinks of me as more or less hand in glove with Mrs. Otway. Or does she not think about my attitude at all? Is it just that she knows in her heart that if Philip saw too much of me he might well change his mind about marrying her?*

She got up with a sigh as Mimi looked in to say rather severely that her dinner was ready. And then, for the third time that evening, the telephone bell rang and, half scared, half eager, Loraine picked up the receiver and said breathlessly, "This is Loraine Darnell speaking."

"Loraine, dear!" It was Mrs. Otway's clear, well- pitched voice that answered. "How fortunate that I caught you in. I've just been talking to Philip and he tells me you'll be free at the weekend. I thought it would be so nice if we went into the country on Sunday and—"

"Mrs. Otway, I'm so sorry!" She had no idea just what was prompting her to say this. "But I remembered after I spoke to Philip that I shan't be free, after all."

"You won't be free?" Disappointment sounded in Mrs. Otway's voice, but, even more, the note of one who was irritated by fresh opposition to some cherished plan. "But couldn't you *make* yourself free?"

"I'm. . .afraid not."

"How disappointing!" She could almost see Mrs. Otway frowning and biting her lip. "Then I wonder what about Saturday. Perhaps we could—"

"I'm almost sure I shall have to be at Florian's on Saturday," Loraine explained quickly. And before Mrs. Otway could query that, she hurried on, "At present, you know, it's difficult to say *when* we shall be free. These are very important weeks, as you know."

"Yes, of course." The sharpness in Mrs. Otway's tone suggested that no one need think she required instruction on the self-evident facts of fashion-house life. "Dear me, how vexing! Philip will be extremely disappointed, Loraine. You're quite sure you couldn't rearrange Sunday's plans?"

"I don't see how I can. I'm so very sorry."

It was quite true. She was sorry. Desperately sorry. But something stronger than herself—whether it was conscience or fear she could not say—stiffened her resolution.

There was a slight pause. Then Mrs. Otway said in a significant sort of voice, "Loraine dear, I think you'll understand me when I say that it could be a very *important* occasion. If I may put it quite crudely, you have made an impression it would be wise to follow up. Can't you really do anything about making Sunday free?"

"I'm very sorry, but no." There was a slight catch in her voice, but she held firmly to her original purpose.

"Well, then there's nothing to do about it." It was obvious that Mrs. Otway found the greatest difficulty in realizing that she was not going to carry her point, after all. "We'll have to see what else—but it's a pity. Timing is so important in these things."

Loraine was tempted to ask shortly, "What things?" But she felt this might involve her in even more difficult conversation. And so she repeated once again—rather inadequately—how sorry she was, and the telephone call ended in an atmosphere of mutual dissatisfaction.

"It isn't *only* because I'm afraid of Elinor's threats," Loraine assured herself as she sat alone later in Paul's charming dining room, doing less than justice to Mimi's admirable dinner. "It's partly the inner conviction that I have no special right to thrust myself into the picture anyway."

If she had been there, naturally and passively, it would have been a different matter. But by a stroke of luck Philip's fiancée had managed to make an issue of the whole thing. She had thrust the onus of aggressive action on Loraine. And aggressive action in this case was simply not justified.

It isn't even as though she's demanding that I do something. She just demands that I do nothing, thought Loraine. *And if she were a nice girl and Mrs. Otway hadn't put ideas into my head, she wouldn't even have had to tell me. I'd have kept out of the way anyway and tried not to make mischief.*

As an academic argument this was splendid. Applied to Philip—and what seemed dangerously like an entanglement with the wrong girl—it had a hollow ring. And for the rest of that evening and quite far into the night Loraine swung to and fro between the two extremes of argument.

But she always came back to the fact that, when she had acted on impulse, she had put off that next meeting with Philip either from fear of Elinor's threats or some instinctive feeling that that was the right thing to do.

The next few days were not happy ones for Loraine. She heard nothing from either Philip or his mother, and, in spite of all the assurances she had given her guardian about being quite happy on her own, she did feel extremely isolated and forlorn.

At work, fortunately, there was little time to think about personal problems. Tension and excitement were now rising to fever pitch and would, Madame Moisant assured her in a moment of cynical candor, presently verge on hysteria.

"Do you mind, *madame*?" Loraine asked with sympathetic curiosity.

"Mind?" repeated the Frenchwoman. "Mind? Why should I mind?"

"Well, you know—I thought you might find it a great strain to have so many excited people to manage. After all, you, too, must have some nerves, I suppose."

"But of steel wire, *petite*," the *directrice* assured her dryly. "Of what good would I be to Monsieur Florian if I sulked and cried and panicked like these others?"

The thought of a weeping and panic-stricken Madame Moisant was so formidable that Loraine shook her head wordlessly.

"I tell you, *ma chère*, I am the only one—but the only one, not excepting Monsieur Florian himself—who must not indulge in emotional crises at this time."

"Does Monsieur Florian. . . panic sometimes?" inquired Loraine, feeling that she could not suggest that he either sulked or wept.

"No. To say that he panics would be to go too far," Madame Moisant conceded. "But he is a great artist, and like all great artists he is entitled to a temperamental outburst or two in times of stress. This one must appreciate if one is to deal with a genius."

"I suppose that's true," Loraine agreed thoughtfully.

"But of course! It is very proper that the mediocre and worthy should have the day-to-day virtues that make for comfortable relationships," Madame Moisant explained with unashamed snobbishness. "But the qualities that make a genius almost inevitably include some which are not easy to live with or work with. One must accept them or, quite simply, go elsewhere. For myself, I would rather work for an interesting fiend than a boring archangel. *Voilà tout.*"

"*Bravo*, Suzanne," said Florian, coming in at that moment. "Something tells me you must be talking about me. But whether as the archangel or the fiend, I'm not sure."

"*Monsieur* knows very well he is not boring," replied Madame Moisant cryptically, which made Florian laugh a good deal and direct a glance of genuine affection at his waspish but devoted *directrice*.

"You must not frighten the little Loraine," he

declared. "She and I have to cooperate very amiably during the next couple of weeks. Isn't that so, *petite*?"

"Yes, *monsieur*," said Loraine obediently.

"Good. Then I hope you will accept with good grace the fact that I shall require you here during most of the weekend."

"Oh, *monsieur*, willingly!" She was almost glad to have the fictitious excuse she had given Mrs. Otway turned into a real one. And she felt something of a fraud when Madame Moisant observed that she was a good child with a very proper attitude toward her work.

In point of fact, the weekend hours of work at the salon proved to be the most exciting she had yet spent, for they were devoted exclusively to the wedding dress, and for the first time Loraine took the full measure of her employer's genius.

Even as early as Marianne's wedding she had already realized that he was a supreme showman, and during the time he had been designing other models for her she had sensed the real artist at work. But now she began to absorb, almost through the pores of her skin, the subtle awareness of what the wedding dress really meant.

Individually, she could see, it was going to be breathtakingly beautiful. But even more, as a climax to the show, it would be stunning. Line and color, design and ravishing materials all combined to state the ultimate in dress beauty, and she felt that one would have to applaud it, even as one would applaud a superb "curtain" at the end of a play.

"*Monsieur*," she ventured to ask, "is this going to be the most beautiful dress you have ever designed?"

"Each wedding dress is the most beautiful I have ever designed," he assured her good-humoredly. "But if you feel nothing could be more beautiful, you will wear it as I would wish."

"That's how I feel," she declared solemnly.

"Then I know I was right to choose you," he said. And this helped her to weather the frightful storm that broke, later in the week, when Lisette discovered that it was Loraine and not she who was to wear the wedding dress.

The news had to be broken eventually, of course, for the opening day was now drawing so near that everyone knew a decision must have been made one way or another. Florian himself made the announcement, curtly and economically, in the dressing room, and forestalled Lisette's angry protests with a mixture of brutality and guile.

"Although for a passing moment I considered you for the part, Lisette, I realized almost immediately that there is nothing bridal about you," he stated frankly. "That is why you have the subtle and provocative evening dresses and the most dramatic cocktail suit in the whole show. These belong to the 'other woman,' a part for which you are supremely—and I may say most attractively—suited. If you are disappointed, pray remember that this is nothing to the disappointment of us all if you had worn the wedding dress and failed."

In her simplicity, Loraine thought this must surely silence and satisfy all. But the moment Florian had left the room Lisette turned on her and upbraided her for being a snake who had insinuated herself into Florian's favor, a thief who had stolen the rights of others and a dull, plain, stupid little simpleton who had made a great mistake if she supposed that she could do such an injury to her, Lisette, and not pay dearly for it.

All this Loraine found very trying, but not so much so as she would have done some weeks ago. And having seized a moment of breathlessness on Lisette's part to state, clearly and categorically, that the choice had nothing to do with anyone but Monsieur Florian, she lapsed into silence, only shrugging occasionally from time to time in a very French gesture of resignation that she had learned from the other girls.

Thunder hung over the dressing room for the rest of that day, however, and by the time she went home Loraine had a headache and felt worn out and depressed. If only something pleasant and soothing and heart lifting would happen! But it was difficult to see what could.

And then, when she arrived home, there was a letter from her guardian. Such a charming, humorous, oddly affectionate letter that Loraine sat down and read it through twice, laughing aloud at one or two of the things he had written, and indescribably comforted by its good humor and normality. It was like a breath of fresh air after the fever and turmoil of the models' dressing room.

Paul explained in the letter that he had had to go to Montreal, as he had expected, and this would make his absence a full three weeks.

But I cannot imagine that in the excitement of the coming dress show, the absence of a mere guardian will even be noticed. I hope you are holding your own with the other competitive young ladies who are to display Florian's creations, and that no one has snatched from you the supreme object of exhibition that I dare not name more precisely.

She thought how nice it was of him to remember, in the midst of his work and his travels, that she was hoping to wear the wedding dress. And since he had given her the address of his Montreal hotel, she wrote back then and there to tell him that all was well with her—a general statement that took no note of the Philip situation—and that "the last act was still hers."

Then, feeling more relaxed and cheered than she could have believed after the tension of the afternoon, she went to bed commendably early and slept dreamlessly until morning.

The next evening Mrs. Otway telephoned, and Loraine could hear immediately that there was a dissatisfied—even a discontented—note in her voice.

"Loraine, dear, what has happened to you?" she wanted to know. "Every day I've expected to hear from you, and Philip tells me he has heard nothing, either."

She thought passingly that there was nothing to prevent Philip himself telephoning if that was how he felt about it. But she said—so truly that she could make the statement convincing—that she had been too busy at Florian's to do much more than take a little food and go to bed each evening on her return from work.

"Darling, I know it must all seem tremendously important to you, especially as it's your first dress show," Mrs. Otway exclaimed plaintively, "but there *are* other things of greater importance in one's life, don't you think?"

"Such as what, Mrs. Otway?" asked Loraine, feeling she could not engage in this rather elaborate double-talk any more.

"Well, if I must speak plainly—" the charming voice became brisker and more decided "—if you neglect Philip like this, you mustn't be surprised if you lose him to Elinor."

"But I have lost him to Elinor," Loraine said gently and firmly. "He is engaged to her, Mrs. Otway. He intends to marry her. I can't enter into any sort of active competition. Surely you must see that?"

"Now, don't be so tiresome, dear child! You can't possibly intend to throw in your hand like that. You love him—you *told* me you do. He was immensely attracted by you as soon as he saw you again. The fact that he had become entangled with the wrong girl is merely something that must be... well... *dis*entangled, as it were. Almost everything you do just now is of vital importance, you silly girl—and there you are behaving as though a few frocks matter more than the happiness of us all."

Loraine resisted the desire to take up this disrespectful way of referring to the Florian collection and said instead, "Mrs. Otway, whatever you or I feel about it I can't make time to see friends just now, even if I want to."

"Not even Philip?"

"N-not even Philip."

"I suppose you call this being dedicated to your work," exclaimed Mrs. Otway impatiently. "All you girls seem to lose your sense of proportion when Florian talks to you. You're making things *very* difficult for me. But I'll do my best to help you out, if you promise me to behave in a more normal way as soon as the opening day is over."

"What do you mean by that exactly?" asked Loraine doubtfully.

"Well, I think I can persuade Philip that I need him home in England for a week or so, in connection with our property there. That will keep him out of that girl's way for a while. Then I shall return in time for the show—and I shall bring Philip with me, you may depend upon that."

"Will Elinor come, too?" inquired Loraine with irresistible curiosity.

"Oh, I suppose so," was the impatient reply. "But if Florian has done his duty by you, Philip will be looking at *you*. Don't you think so?"

Loraine was silent for a moment. She thought of what Florian had said of the impression she would create in his wedding dress. And in spite of all the conscientious arguments she had been detailing to herself lately, she sensed for a moment the unspeakable rapture it would be if she did indeed see in Philip's eyes the look that told her he had forgotten everyone else but her.

"Are you still there, Loraine?"

"Yes, Mrs. Otway."

"And did you hear my question?"

"Yes. I can only say that Florian has designed some wonderful things for me. The kind of things I—I would like Philip to see me wear."

"Ah, that's better!" Mrs. Otway gave an exclamation of satisfaction. "Well now, darling, you leave it to me. I'll keep Philip in England during the next dangerous week or so. Then we must rely on your making a tremendous impression on him in the new Florian fashions. And *this* time you must follow up the advantage. We can't afford to waste *two* good openings.''

Loraine very much disliked the use of *we* in this connection and the determined assumption that Mrs. Otway and she were firmly linked in an attempt to remodel Philip's life for him. But it was useless to argue just then. And—why not face the truth—her heart beat with fresh irrepressible hope at the thought of what that dramatic dress show could—might—do for her.

So she said, ''I'll be very glad for Philip to see me at the show. And—and if he shows unmistakably that *I* am the one he really loves, then I can't pretend that I'll do nothing about it.''

''Splendid! I knew you'd look at things more sensibly if we had a little talk,'' Mrs. Otway declared cheerfully. ''If I don't see you again before the opening day, dear— and that's probably the best way to arrange it if we can—then good luck.''

And she rang off, obviously in a much better frame of mind than when she had begun the conversation.

Loraine could not contain her excitement and her rising hopes. She walked softly about the room, clasping and unclasping her hands, while she savored the wonderful thought that, without any intervention on her part, Philip would meet her again in circumstances that would constitute the perfect test of his real feelings.

When I walk past in the wedding dress I shall know *how he feels,* she told herself. *If he loves me, I shall see it in his face, even if he only discovers it himself in that moment.*

She was so certain of this, so supremely sure that she could leave the issue to this final test, that suddenly she was quite calm about it all. And she suffered only a momentary disappointment the next evening when Mimi greeted her on her very late return with the information that a Mr. Otway had telephoned an hour ago to say goodbye before leaving for England.

''Oh, Mimi! Did he say when he was leaving?''

"In half an hour's time. Half an hour from when he telephoned," explained the exact Mimi.

"Then he'll have gone by now."

"Yes. He'll have gone by now."

"Oh, well. It doesn't matter really. I'll be seeing him on his return," Loraine said. And she smiled such a smile of secret joy that even the unimaginative Mimi gave her a reflective look before returning to her own affairs.

After that Loraine was able to devote her every thought to her work, secure in the knowledge that Philip's affairs had been miraculously held in suspense—if one could regard Mrs. Otway's interference in the light of a miracle, that was—until the great, the longed-for day of the new collection.

And not even Florian himself was pinning more radiant hopes upon that day than she was, Loraine thought.

Then, two days before the vital date, her guardian returned, heralded by a telegram, which Loraine found waiting for her on her return from work, saying that he was flying direct from Montreal.

She had been sent home comparatively early that day with instructions to rest, as the following day would include the evening showing of the collection to the work girls.

Mimi handed her the telegram as soon as she came in with the remark that *monsieur* should be arriving at the air terminal anytime now.

"Oh, then I shall go and meet him!" exclaimed Loraine. "How lovely that I came home in time." And without even waiting to put on a hat, she ran downstairs, hailed a passing taxi and drove to the air terminal arriving in the big hall at the precise moment that he appeared at the luggage counter.

At the sight of his tanned familiar figure she felt the most extraordinary rush of relief and reassurance. And she cried, "Paul!" and ran to him, her eyes bright, her hair a little windblown and a welcoming smile on her lips.

"Why, Loraine!" He turned with an exclamation of pleasure and actually took her in his arms and kissed her.

It was something of a surprise to both of them. But a nice surprise, Loraine thought, and she hugged him with uninhibited warmth and said, "I'm so *glad* to see you back."

"Are you, dear child?" He laughed, but again it was a pleased laugh. "Well, I'm extraordinarily glad to see you. I think it's the first time I've ever had someone come to welcome me home."

He linked her arm in his and left the collecting of the luggage to a porter as they made their way to the taxi rank.

"You're a bit thinner," he commented critically, "and just a trifle pale. Has that brute, Florian, been overworking you?"

"No more than all the rest," she assured him with a laugh. "And no more than I was willing to accept. We're all *living* for the opening of the new collection, the day after tomorrow. But tell me about your trip."

So he told her quite a lot about his visit to Canada, adding personal details and reactions that made something much more intimate of their conversation than had been the case before he went away. And she said suddenly, "You've changed somehow."

"*I* have?" He laughed. "Nonsense! People of my age don't change."

"Well, then, perhaps I have," she said slowly.

"It could be." He touched her cheek lightly and rather charmingly. "Or perhaps you've just come to know me better. I'm rather a tiresome difficult chap to know, I suppose. Not at all like the simple straightforward creature you are yourself."

"Am I simple and straightforward?"

"Yes, of course. In the nicest way possible. That's one of the most satisfying things about you. Something like truth itself." He smiled at her suddenly troubled face. "Don't look so solemn. It's very rare and delightful to be without deceit or guile of any kind."

"Oh," said Loraine, and felt simply dreadful, because she could not possibly tell him how much guile—not to say deceit—she had practiced in her determination to keep from him the fact that she was in love with the man he probably considered to be his most hated enemy.

Fortunately they arrived home at this moment, and she was saved any further embarrassing discussion on the subject of truth and its attractions.

But she thought, *I hope he's not going to dislike and despise me when he finds out the real situation. But I can't think about that now. I can't think about anything except how Philip will look when he sees me wear the wedding dress. If everything is all right in that moment, I'll ask nothing more. Just let everything—everything—go smoothly on that day, and I can deal with whatever comes later.*

They dined together in excellent humor. But he sent her to bed early, with the reminder that now there was a guardian to look after her interests again, and he could not allow any ward of his to look pale and tired with so great an occasion drawing near.

It was singularly pleasant to feel in someone's care again, she decided, and altogether she was genuinely happy to have him home, even though some obvious complications loomed ahead.

The next day included all the usual minor crises and scenes, with the addition of last-minute nerves. But everything smoothed out miraculously for the show that was given for the work girls, and here Loraine had her first taste of real personal success.

It had been one thing to show someone else's dresses in the old collection. It was quite another to be wearing—perhaps *expressing* was the word—the designs that had actually been created for her.

She drew rapturous applause from the solid group of girls who had been responsible for making her outfits. But this, Madame Moisant had explained to her, would happen in any case, for approval at this particular show was strictly of a partisan variety. What was really surprising was that she caused approving comments, and even some applause, from those who had had no hand in making her dresses. And this, she was given to understand, was praise indeed.

Even at this final preview, as it were, Florian did not allow the wedding dress to go on show. But Loraine went home cheered by the thought of her success and by a special word of praise from Florian. Strained and preoccupied though he looked, he had given her a quick smile at the end and said, "Tomorrow should be a great day."

Paul had evidently been detained late on his own affairs. Which was just as well, Loraine thought, for Mrs. Otway telephoned quite late in the evening, and it scared her even to think what complications would have arisen if her guardian had been at home and taken the call. She must somehow insist that, in future, calls be made only to the salon, however inexplicable that might seem.

Or perhaps, after tomorrow, she would not have to worry about that—or anything else.

"Darling, I just wanted you to know that we're back and *so* much looking forward to tomorrow," Mrs. Otway assured her. "We shall be in the main room, right in the front row, ready to cheer you on."

"All three of you?" Loraine could not help inquiring.

"All three of us will be there," Mrs. Otway agreed, but in a slightly repressive sort of tone that suggested she took no responsibility for any cheering on Elinor's part.

"I'm so glad. I think you'll like it," Loraine said with happy understatement. Then she hastily said goodbye and rang off because she heard her guardian's key in the door.

Paul teased her a little that evening, saying that he and Mimi must remember that they had a prima donna on their hands, and that if she wanted to throw a tantrum before her debut, that would be quite in order.

But he was kind, too, and again saw that she went to

bed in good time. And she found, the following morning, that he intended to take her down by car to the salon.

"You simply can't walk on such a morning," he declared.

And although it made her nervous to think of him anywhere near the scene of action even so early in the morning, she could not but be touched by his forethought. She was, however, really feeling nervous and keyed up by now, and she sat almost wordless beside him as they drove through the light haze of a perfect summer morning.

When they drove up outside Florian's, Paul kissed her cheek lightly and said, "Good luck, Loraine. I'll see you later."

"I expect it will be very much later," she warned him as she got out of the car and stood on the pavement smiling at him. "We shall be here to all hours tonight. But I'll tell you all about it sometime this evening."

"Sometime this evening be blowed!" he told her cheerfully. "I'm coming to the show. You didn't think I'd miss your big moment, did you?"

If the House of Florian had collapsed behind her, she could not have been more stunned or horrified.

"You're coming...to the show?" she gasped, passing in rapid, nightmare review scenes of him meeting Elinor...Mrs. Otway...Philip.

"Certainly! Florian kindly sent me a ticket yesterday. Don't look so scared. You're going to be splendid, I'm sure.",

And with a final reassuring wave of his hand, he drove off, leaving Loraine staring after him.

CHAPTER SEVEN

WHAT SHALL I DO? What shall I do, thought Loraine distractedly. *Paul* can't *come to the show. It will spoil absolutely everything. The whole situation is so delicately poised. A meeting—any sort of showdown—would be utter disaster! Oh, why didn't I think of this? But how could I? How could I guess for one moment that Florian would send Paul a ticket? He had no* right to.

Terrified by the crisis, blinded to everything but her own predicament, Loraine really did think it monstrous of Florian to issue a ticket—at least, this particular ticket—to his own dress show.

And suddenly, realizing that she was still standing stock-still on the pavement while time was running out, she whirled and rushed through the famous portals, across the boutique and up the stairs.

Ordinarily she would have stopped here and gone along to the models' dressing room. But consumed by a fever of panic and distress, she ran on, up to the top floor where Florian had his own working quarters.

She was not even thinking of the enormity of what she was doing, or that on this day—one of the two most important of the year—even Madame Moisant handled Florian with kid gloves. She knocked on the door of his office and marched in almost before his nervous, slightly irritable voice bade her enter.

"Monsieur Florian—"

"Go away," he said impatiently. "I want no one to disturb me just now. You have no right up here, in any case. You should be downstairs dressing."

"But *monsieur*—"

"Talk to Madame Moisant!" he thundered in a voice

she had never heard from him before. "I am not interested." And he turned his back on her and went over to the window, where he stood drumming his fingers moodily on the pane.

She could not imagine where she found the courage to go on. It must be something to do with sheer desperation, she supposed. But even she herself was astonished when she heard her voice, rather thin and high, say, "If you want me to wear your wedding dress, *monsieur*, you had better listen."

If she had bitten him he could not have been more astounded. He turned slowly and looked at her—a look that was reputed to be able to make a duchess wilt.

"What did you say?" asked Florian quietly and incredulously.

"I said," repeated Loraine shakily, "that if you want me to wear your wedding dress, you had better listen to me."

"I am listening," said Florian with such withering chill that she felt the salt taste of fresh panic in her mouth.

"It's about the ticket you sent Paul—my guardian," she stammered, at which he cast a glance upward as though calling on heaven to witness what a dress designer had to put up with.

"It's vital that he shouldn't use it."

"Vital to whom?" inquired Florian with a sort of savage calm.

"To me. The girl who is going to wear your wedding dress."

"Stop trying to blackmail me, *mademoiselle*." Florian was suddenly in complete command of the situation again. "I am aware of your power on this day, even if I sack you tomorrow. What is it you are trying to ask of me?"

"Monsieur Florian—" she actually wrung her hands in her distress "—I'm not trying to blackmail you. But Philip is coming here today. Almost everything for me depends on his seeing me, without complication or distraction, in the wedding dress. Now you've arranged that Paul should be here, too. They're deadly enemies. Neither knows I am anything to the other, or that I even *know* the other. And, as though that were not enough, Philip is bringing his fiancée—the girl who jilted Paul.''

"What do you expect *me* to do about this ridiculous tangle?" inquired her employer coldly, and as he passed his hand over his face and hair, she realized suddenly how pale and strained he looked. "Am I supposed to meet your guardian at the door—on this day of all days—and insult him by telling him I do not want him at my dress show, after all?"

"N-no. But do *something*, Monsieur Florian. Everyone says you're such a clever and ingenious man. Surely you can think of some solution? They mustn't meet. That's all. *They must not meet*."

He stared at her wordlessly for perhaps half a minute. Then he said almost conversationally, "I could wring your neck with pleasure. But since I cannot allow myself even the indulgence of sacking you today, I will help you instead."

"Oh, *monsieur*!"

"Don't thank me." He held up his hand peremptorily. "It would be an insult after holding a pistol at my head like this. Where is Monsieur Philippe sitting?"

"I—I don't know. Oh, yes, I do! I remember now. Mrs. Otway said they would be in the front row in the main room."

"Very well, then. I will have your guardian met at the door—you must excuse me if I do not immediately undertake this task myself," he added with unexpectedly heavy irony for him, "and I will arrange for him to be seated in the long corridor."

"But suppose, in spite of this—"

"I will suppose nothing," stated Florian with brutal finality. "I have offered you a solution. It must suffice. And now, if you do not leave me, I will have you removed and Lisette shall wear the wedding dress and spoil the show."

It seemed inappropriate to say "Thank you, *monsieur*" at that point. So Loraine silently withdrew, sorry that she could not express gratitude even for this limited help, and, on legs that seemed strangely hollow, she tottered down to her proper floor.

Here Madame Moisant greeted her with hardly suppressed fury.

"Where have you been?" she inquired in the tone of one who longed to administer a sharp slap to a child but feared this might result in a screaming fit that would spoil the party. "You should have been here ten minutes ago."

"I know. I'm very sorry. I was speaking to Monsieur Florian," Loraine said truthfully.

"To Monsieur Florian?" Madame Moisant's voice rose to a squeak of incredulous horror. "One does not speak to Monsieur Florian on the opening day."

"Well, I did," said Loraine simply.

"Did he send for you?"

"No. I went to speak to him on my own account."

"On your own— You must be mad!" exclaimed the *directrice*.

"Yes, I think perhaps I am," Loraine replied unexpectedly. "And if you question me any further, Madame Moisant, I shall probably scream and try to run up the wall."

One of the facets of Madame Moisant's genius was to know when to impose and when to relax discipline. She gave one measuring glance at Loraine.

Then she said mildly, "We will talk no more of this, *petite*—nor of going mad. There is time for everything if we organize well. You will take a mouthful of wine and get dressed in your first number, and today you will be such a success that no one will remember any earlier foolishness."

And so she arranged it, though she allowed herself the luxury of muttering to her favorite fitter that the British were the most unpredictable race on earth.

"One says they have no temperament," she added

bitterly. "This is true of the typical beefy Britisher. But if they do have temperament then nothing can stand in their path. This is perhaps why they win wars."

"True, *madame*," agreed the fitter, who cared nothing about the Britishers or their wars but was devoted to Madame Moisant.

Imprisoned, as it were, in the dressing room, Loraine had no further opportunity of seeing if Florian really carried out what he had promised or whether, in fact, the simple ruse had even partially solved her problem.

But just before the show was about to begin, she persuaded Madame Moisant to let her look through the small peephole that commanded a view of the main room. And there, sure enough, sitting in the front row, was Philip, flanked on either side by his mother and Elinor.

Of Paul there was no sign at all, so presumably he was now safely seated in the long corridor. Whether he and Philip had met, at any rate passingly, or what would happen afterward, she could not say. At least she would not be called upon to parade before both men at the same time, with Elinor also looking on. And the relief of this realization was so overwhelming that suddenly she found she was quite calm, relaxed and ready to play her part.

"Well...we are not going mad, after all, eh?" Madame Moisant glanced briefly at Loraine's more tranquil expression, like a general giving special attention to his weakest troops before battle.

"Oh, no! I'm sorry, *madame*. Everything is all right now. I think perhaps I was a bit crazy with stage fright," Loraine said contritely.

"Very possibly. It is not unusual," agreed the *directrice*. Then she consulted her watch and asked, "Are you ready, Lisette?" of Lisette, who was to open the show.

"Yes, *madame*." Lisette looked exaggeratedly calm, just to show that *she* was no amateur suffering from nerves.

Then Madame Moisant moved over to her vantage point, picked up her hand microphone and announced, "*Numero vingt-et-un*. Numbaire Twenty-one."

The show had begun.

The numbering was not consecutive, but each girl knew, even without the summoning crook of Madame Moisant's finger, when her turn came.

Loraine's first appearance—in a smoke-blue *tailleur* with infinitely clever touches of mink—did not come until the show had been in progress for ten minutes. Then, as Madame Moisant's rather harsh voice announced her first number, she stepped out onto the small semicircular stage with the strangest feeling of walking toward her fate.

She was not really nervous now. Only immensely keyed up and excited, though outwardly calm. She was still fully aware of everything that this moment meant to her, Loraine, personally. But with another part of her— the part that was to make her one of the most successful models even Florian ever discovered—she saw the whole thing in terms of theater. And like an actress making the most of a dramatic entrance, she turned slowly, nodded faintly at no one and at everyone, and then made her way along the narrow raised platform that ran down the center of the main salon.

As she passed Philip and his mother, she gave them a vivid smiling glance—just enough to show that she was a living, intensely human girl and not simply a clothes prop—completed her walk, turned and retraced her steps and then moved out and along the corridor, just as the next number was announced and the next girl appeared on the circular stage.

Almost at the end of the corridor and near the head of the stairs she saw Paul. And beside him sat Florian himself.

She could have laughed aloud in her relief and in the realization that Florian had been even better than his word. Although he might not actually have met Paul when he came in, at least he was giving some personal attention to him, and Loraine might rest assured that he would see to it there was no crisis.

The smile she had given Philip had been charming enough. But the smile she bestowed upon Florian—and by a slight extension, on her guardian, too—was of such feeling and beauty that more than one voice was heard to declare that this new model of Florian's was about to steal the show.

Paul himself looked as though he shared this view, and Loraine could not but be touched and pleased by the half-incredulous delight with which he surveyed her, almost as though he saw her for the first time and liked beyond measure what he saw.

Florian, for his part, looked coolly back at her. But although on his worn clever face there was that curiously boyish smile that appeared in moments of sudden pleasure or great tension, she had the feeling that the smile was not meant for her.

At last her first tour was over and she was back in the dressing room, where the elegant languor of display gave place immediately to the feverish activity of changing into the next model. And from then onward, in spite of expert organization and split-second timing, the tempo increased cruelly, and the alternation of leisurely appearances and backstage rush sharpened tempers and tightened nerves.

Before the show was half over, however, the indefinable breath of success began to stir the over-heated atmosphere of the salon. And as the stunning evening dresses, which were perhaps the finest expression of Florian's genius, followed each other in superb procession, this breath grew to a strong breeze and then almost to a gale, expressed in the continual outbursts of applause and the exclamations of delight.

Loraine had one of her greatest successes in a quite simple dress of pale daffodil organdy worn with an immense-skirted dramatic evening coat of magnificent green satin. And as though the clapping and general approval were not enough, she actually heard Philip say softly as she passed, "Oh, lovely...lovely!"

She was not quite sure if he spoke to her or to himself. But she did know that the exclamation was forced from him by some feeling that he could not possibly suppress.

This was her last model before the wedding dress. And when she returned to the dressing room, she found Florian himself waiting to see her arrayed in his final inspiration.

Those who were no longer required to show the last few numbers crowded around to comment and admire. And Odette—the model who had been longest with Florian and now showed the incredibly elegant clothes designed for the not so young—said frankly, "It is the most beautiful you have ever designed, *monsieur*."

"You think so, Odette?" He gave her that quick boyish smile. "In the very last moment I never know if it is good or not."

"It is superb and yet touching beyond belief. Like faint mist at dawn, with that glow of shell pink just showing through the white."

"And there's dew on it, too," said Loraine, softly touching the folds of the skirt, where an occasional *paillette* lent sparkle to the breathtaking clouds of tulle.

"True," said Florian. But she could not tell from his tone if they were really on speaking terms, or whether she had been forgiven for her outrageous piece of insubordination before the show began.

And then Madame Moisant gave a peremptory gesture and Loraine heard her make the last announcement, which heralded the entry of the wedding dress.

"Slowly," whispered Florian, "slowly. And remember that now you are not a model showing a dress, but a bride going toward her happiness."

"Yes, *monsieur*," she whispered in return, and her voice was faintly tremulous. Then she parted the curtains and stood there before Philip—for the others did not count—in all the touching glory of the wedding dress.

With instinctive artistry, she made no conventional turn. She just stood there for almost a minute, her hands lightly clasped against her breast, her wide eyes looking with half-timid rapture toward the future. Then, in the stunned silence that had greeted her entrance, she moved slowly forward. And as she did so, the applause broke out like a thunderclap.

She was aware that, incredibly, half the audience had risen to its feet and were waving their programs in tribute. But she moved slowly on as though she saw nothing...nothing but the shining future in front of her.

She had meant to break that rapt glance when she reached Philip and look at him with a faint smile that would tell him that this was especially for him. But in some inexplicable way she could not free herself from the spell that she herself had created.

To look at anyone at close range would be to shatter the mood of rapturous isolation that was the keynote of her impression. She had no idea that, in that moment, she completely surrendered her private interests to the demands of artistic integrity. She only knew that she must continue to look ahead, which she did.

"The child is wonderful...wonderful," she heard Mrs. Otway say excitedly. "Did you ever see anything so lovely, Philip?"

And she thought he said, "Never." But she could not be quite sure because of the pandemonium around her.

She moved through it all, and on the return journey, too, serene and rapt. Then she was out in the corridor, looking down the full length of it, and perfectly naturally, her wide-eyed glance rested on her guardian.

It was the most extraordinary experience. As though something or someone awoke her from a trance. And as she awoke, she smiled.

He got to his feet. He was not the only one. But he gave the impression of rising in the presence of something a little unearthly, and he did not shout or wave his program. He did not even clap. He just looked at her, incredulously. And as she passed he said softly, "You darling!"

She could not have said why, but that brought the tears to her eyes. And although she was now too well disciplined to allow them to fall, by the time she returned to the dressing room, tears were trembling on her lashes.

"Not on the wedding dress! Not on the wedding dress!" exclaimed Madame Moisant, thrusting her handkerchief into her hand. "But you were splendid, *petite*, splendid. Now blow your nose and be cheerful, for all is well."

Loraine obeyed submissively, while everyone crowded around to congratulate her, with the exception of Lisette, who stood aloof and remarked that they were there to display Monsieur Florian's dresses and not to play theater, which was what Loraine had done.

"It is natural that you should be jealous, Lisette," said Madame Moisant genially. "But you are stupid to show it. Now take off the dress, Loraine."

"One moment, *madame*!" Florian came in—having torn himself away from a storm of congratulations outside—and as the girls fell back respectfully, he came up to Loraine.

"Thank you, *chérie*," he said, and taking her hand, he kissed it.

"Oh, *monsieur*!" To her dismay, Loraine felt quite tearful again. "Am I...am I forgiven?"

"For what, *petite*?"

"Oh, you *know*! For the—the awful things I said to you before the show," Loraine exclaimed remorsefully.

"Once success is assured, I forget everything that happened before the show," Florian assured her, his gray eyes glinting with amusement.

"Oh, *monsieur*, how generous of you!"

"But perhaps I should remember to tell you that your guardian has already safely left."

"*Left?*" Inexplicably, she was stunned with disappointment. "Left...without a word to me? Oh, but I wanted—"

"You wanted to make sure that he and Monsieur Philippe did not meet at any cost," her employer reminded her dryly.

"Yes, of course." She tried to remember how unspeakably important that was.

"By careful arrangement, I kept them apart before the show. And by assuring your guardian there was no chance of speaking to you, I sent him briskly on his way once more. I hope," said Florian a trifle maliciously, "that you are properly grateful."

"Oh, I...I am. But did he *want* to come and speak to me?"

"Very much."

"Oh, I wish you had let him!"

"At the risk of his running into Monsieur Philippe?"

She did not answer that immediately. She stared at Florian instead, as though she had recalled or discovered something that had given her a great shock. Then she said, quite irrelevantly, "I didn't look at Philip after all. I—I looked at Paul."

"Ah," said the great designer softly, "that is indeed interesting. Now take off the wedding dress. You have a busy day in front of you, and I think your friend, Mrs. Otway, is hoping to have a word with you."

He left her then, and she carefully divested herself of the wedding dress with the brisk assistance of one of the principal *vendeuses*, who already wanted her to come and display a couple of her models for a customer.

"They are for a prospective bride," she explained to Loraine, "so she may want several designs for her trousseau. But not the wedding dress, I think. That would not be her style."

"Who is she?" inquired Loraine, pausing in the act of changing to a midnight-blue cocktail dress.

"Miss Roye. Her future mother-in-law is a very good customer of ours."

"I know them," Loraine said briefly, and she accompanied the *vendeuse* to one of the larger fitting rooms, where she found not only Elinor and Mrs. Otway but Philip, too.

They were all congratulatory—even Elinor in a cool, impersonal sort of way—but it was Mrs. Otway who did most of the talking. Philip was quite extraordinarily silent once he had expressed his admiration of Loraine's part in the show, and she had the impression that he was deeply troubled.

Well, perhaps that was the way it had to be. It could hardly be easy to watch one's fiancée choosing things for her trousseau if one had just made the shattering discovery that one loved someone else.

Only... *was* that the discovery he had made?

As she went through the motions of being intelligently interested in Elinor's choice, Loraine found herself desperately trying to decide what that moody silence of Philip's meant.

In all her hopes and anticipations, she had never faced the fact that she might be no nearer the truth even when the great dress show was over. But then, of course, when it came to the point, she had not put the issue to the test.

She could hardly believe it now. And certainly she could not explain it to herself. Why, *why* had she not looked at him at that vital moment when she appeared before him in the wedding dress? That was to be the test, and on the result of it she was to be able to base all her future actions.

Instead of which she had not even looked at him. She had looked at Paul instead.

And Paul had said, "You darling!" and brought the tears to her eyes. Which had nothing whatever to do with the present situation but seemed curiously important, all the same.

"What do you think, Philip?" Elinor turned suddenly to her fiancé. "We haven't heard your opinion. And if you're going to live with these dresses, you'd better have some choice in the matter. How do you like the blue cocktail dress?"

"It looks lovely to me," Philip said slowly. But he looked straight at Loraine as he said it.

"You don't feel it's a trifle *ingénue* for you, dear?" That was Mrs. Otway being disparagingly helpful. And not for the first time, Loraine felt unhappy and ashamed to be in any sort of alliance with her, however involuntary.

"I hadn't thought so," replied Elinor dryly. "Would you like me to have it, Philip?"

"If it pleases you."

"But I was asking if it pleased *you*," Elinor said gently and firmly.

Philip had always, in Loraine's experience, been completely at ease in any situation. But now he actually looked faintly harassed as he laughed impatiently and said, "If you like it, my dear, I think you should have it."

"Which means that you don't like it very much yourself?" she pressed him.

"I must confess I find these dress shows rather more confusing than you women seem to do." Philip shrugged but made an effort to show something of his usual good temper. "Once I've seen someone in a dress, particularly a clever dress, it seems odd to me to transfer it to someone else. For me, that's Loraine's dress and—"

"I know just what you mean!" his mother cut in brightly. "But then that's partly the clever way our little Loraine wears her things. They become essentially *her*. I thought that was particularly so with the wedding dress, didn't you?"

"Yes," said Philip without elaboration, and for a couple of seconds that monosyllable seemed to hang significantly in the air.

Loraine found that she could not look at the other girl. In this moment, which should have been her own moment of triumph, the thing she was most aware of was the mortification of her rival and, from the bottom of her heart, she was sorry for Elinor.

"Perhaps," murmured the *vendeuse* tactfully, "the models worn by one of the other girls—one that he does not know personally—might please *monsieur* more. I will see."

She melted away discreetly, and Loraine supposed she was expected to do the same. But she stood there for a moment longer. And then, just as she was secretly pitying Elinor for her defenseless state, the other girl drew the most dangerous weapon she possessed.

"It would be hard on Florian if all the menfolk thought as you did," she told Philip with an almost affectionate and indulgent little laugh. "If no one wanted to see Loraine's models on anyone but Loraine, who would buy them? Even the man she lives with could hardly be as generous as that."

"The— What did you say?" Philip turned on his fiancée almost fiercely. "Who on earth are you talking about?"

"Why, Paul Cardine, of course." Elinor opened her eyes quite wide. "Didn't you know? But you *must* know that Loraine is living there in his flat. He calls her his ward, I believe."

CHAPTER EIGHT

FOR THE SECOND TIME that day Loraine found herself the cause of a stunned silence. But this was very different from the enraptured hush that had greeted the appearance of the wedding dress. This was something so appalling and so totally unexpected that she felt herself pale.

Then Philip said with a deadly sort of calm, "Are you mad, Elinor? Loraine is one of our closest friends, and it's simply impossible for you to make such a statement about her."

"But she *is* living in Paul Cardine's flat," reiterated his fiancée, unmoved. "Ask her, if you don't believe me, or ring her up at the telephone number she gave you. That's Paul's number. I should know!" And she laughed shortly.

"Loraine...." Philip turned almost appealingly to her, and she saw him start slightly—perhaps with shock at the sight of her pale face and curiously guilty demeanor.

"Paul Cardine is my guardian," Loraine said in a queer, breathy little voice. "I do live in his flat. But Elinor's implication of—of anything else is, of course, ridiculous."

"What am I supposed to have implied?" murmured Elinor with a deprecating little shrug. But Philip was not even looking at her. He was still looking in incredulous dismay at Loraine.

"But, for heaven's sake, why didn't you tell me? Why this disquieting mystery?"

"There was no mystery," Loraine began desperately. But before she could say any more, or in any way remove the unfortunate impression that Elinor had created, the *vendeuse* came hurrying back into the room accompanied by Madame Moisant, who immediately addressed herself apologetically to Mrs. Otway.

"You must excuse us, dear Madame Otway, but Loraine is needed by Monsieur Florian. The wedding dress is all ready to be photographed for the press. In any case, I understand that Mademoiselle Roye would rather see some models on one of the other girls."

This was not exactly what Mademoiselle Roye had indicated, but she immediately said accommodatingly that she would be interested to see some of Lisette's models. And, before Mrs. Otway could protest, or Philip insist on finishing the discussion—which would have been useless in any case—Loraine was whisked away and once more arrayed in the gorgeous wedding dress.

No form of mockery could have been more cruel, and it was all she could do to hide her unhappiness and despair. But she was, after all, a vital part of Florian's great day. There was no question of her allowing her inconsiderable little private affairs to interfere with the natural course of events. She had tried that once and been forgiven. She could hardly expect to be indulged any further.

"You need not look so serious, *petite*," Florian told her. "A bride should show happiness, even if she is also awed and *un peu exaltée*."

So Loraine did her best to look as an awed and happy bride should look. And she must, she supposed, be more of an actress than she had known because everyone seemed very well satisfied and a great many photographs were taken.

Then she was seized on immediately to display the yellow-and-green evening ensemble and two of her day dresses for a young South American heiress, to whom time and money were apparently of equally little importance. By the time Loraine had finished that assignment, there was no sign of the Otways or Elinor and, on inquiry, she found they had gone at least half an hour ago.

There was nothing she could do about it. This day— or what was left of it—belonged to Florian. And all that afternoon, and quite far into the evening, she patiently posed and changed and posed again—for customers, for photographers, for Florian himself when he required her in order to reinforce some viewpoint he wished to put over to the press.

She was deadly tired by the end. So tired that it was difficult to say if her head or her back or her legs ached most. But, far more than any physical ache, was the dull, despairing knowledge that, on this day to which she had pinned so many bright and secret hopes, she had only succeeded in creating doubt and dismay in Philip's mind.

There will be a chance to explain, she kept on telling herself, in the intervals of smiling and looking bright and attentive. *Of course there will! He didn't really believe anything questionable about my presence in Paul's apartment. It's only a matter of having a quiet talk with him and explaining everything.*

But she knew uneasily that, all the while she was rooted here in Florian's salon, time was going on, unfortunate impressions were being confirmed and Elinor was undoubtedly using every advantage she had so ruthlessly snatched.

It was over at last, though one or two of the girls were actually going on to show their models at a midnight charity affair.

"You have no need to droop and look pathetic," Lisette told her briskly. "You are not wanted anymore and can go home. Me, I am still needed for further display."

"Good luck to you," replied Loraine, who knew she was supposed to feel mortified by this slight. "My only concern is how to *get* home. If I can't pick up a taxi, I think I'll drop in my tracks."

"You cannot get your boyfriend to fetch you in his car?" asked Lisette contemptuously.

"No," said Loraine, not bothering to inquire who her boyfriend was supposed to be.

But when she came out into the street, the most beautiful welcome sight met her eye. Paul's car was drawn up by the curb and he was sitting at the wheel, patiently reading an evening newspaper.

"Oh, *Paul!*" With what strength she had left she ran across the pavement to him.

"Hello, darling." He leaned over and opened the door for her. "Slip in. I expect you're pretty whacked, aren't you?"

"Nearly dead," she assured him. "How did you *know* I needed a lift so badly and would be coming out just at this moment?"

"I guessed it would be a tough day and reckoned I'd better come and wait for you."

"You angel! How long have you been waiting?"

He glanced at his watch and said in some surprise, "About an hour, I suppose."

"About an hour! How kind of you to waste your evening like that."

"I didn't think of it as a wasted evening," he told her with a quick smile. "I couldn't wait to tell you how wonderful you were, Loraine. Florian wouldn't let me have so much as a word with you when the show was over, and I've been bottling it up ever since. I had no idea I was harboring a minor genius in my home."

"Don't exaggerate!" she said, and laughed. But she was infinitely pleased really, and oddly soothed.

"No exaggeration," he assured her. "It wasn't only the natural grace and charm, Loraine. It was the way you made almost a stage role of every design. You were different every time. Did you know?"

"N-no. I don't think I did."

"It was fascinating. I wasn't the only one who noticed. Everyone was talking about you. I was bursting with pride and couldn't help telling several people you were my ward."

"Paul, you didn't!"

"Indeed, I did. Do you mind?"

"No, of course not. But somehow I can't imagine your doing anything so—so naive and nice."

"Good Lord!" He made a face. "Was I actually being naive?"

"Well, no. Perhaps not. Perhaps you were just being nice," she told him. And she put her head against his shoulder and rested very contentedly there.

He made no more conversation on the short drive home, for which she was glad. She was able to think about Philip and how she could explain everything to him, which made her draw a troubled sigh once, though, inexplicably, she already felt less distracted.

Paul glanced at her when she sighed but still he said nothing. And even when they got home, he treated her a little as though she were an invalid, which was hardly less than bliss after the day she had had.

He made her have her supper on a small table, which he drew up beside her armchair, and he gave her a glass of some very special wine, which made her feel exquisitely warmed and soothed.

"Feeling better now?" he inquired when, her meal finished, she leaned back in her chair and smiled at him.

"Heaps better. You're the best of guardians."

He actually flushed slightly at that, which touched her as well as faintly amused her, and reminded her forcibly of the way he had looked at her when she walked past him in the wedding dress.

"You really did enjoy the dress show, then?" She put out her hand and lightly patted his arm.

"Enormously. Particularly your part in it. Florian was delighted with you, too, wasn't he?"

"I think so."

"There was no doubt of it! He was muttering to himself in a satisfied way each time you came into view."

"Really?" She looked interested. "Even before the sensation of the wedding dress?"

"Certainly. But that doesn't surprise you, surely?"

"It does rather. He was very cross with me just before the show began, and I wasn't sure at which point he forgave me."

"Cross with you? Whatever for?" Paul looked rather annoyed on her behalf.

"Oh, well...." She remembered suddenly that she could not possibly explain in detail. "There are lots of ups and downs on a day like this."

"I gathered as much," he said unexpectedly. "What went wrong, Loraine?"

"Nothing went wrong," she assured him quickly. "What made you think so?"

"The moment you appeared, when I went to fetch you this evening, I saw that something had clouded the earlier radiance."

"That was just tiredness."

"No, dear, it wasn't. I wish you'd tell me."

She wished she could. She wished it so intensely that she could not keep the eager impulse to confide in him from showing in her face.

"Come on," he urged her, half laughing, half serious. "What are guardians for if they can't offer counsel and consolation when things go wrong?"

"I don't think I can. It's so difficult...."

And then the utter longing to tell *someone*—to shift even a small amount of the worry that was weighing her down—became too strong to resist, and she said in a rather small voice, "You won't like me very much when I tell you."

"How do you know? It would take quite something to make me stop liking you."

"Would it, Paul?" Again her hand went out to touch his arm in that light appealing gesture. "You once said I was so straight and truthful. I haven't been absolutely straight with you."

"Haven't you?" He frowned, but in thought rather than anger. "About Florian, you mean?"

"Oh, no! It's nothing to do with Florian, except indirectly, this morning. It's to do with Elinor and the man she's now engaged to."

"With Elinor?" He stiffened suddenly and his expression changed, so that he looked aloof and on guard. "What on earth do you know about her?"

"She was there this morning, you know."

"Yes, I know," he said unexpectedly. "I caught a glimpse of her before the show began. That was one reason why I didn't stay to speak to you afterward. Florian assured me that I would have to hang about indefinitely before I got a word with you, and I didn't feel inclined to risk that."

"He was there, too," Loraine said slowly.

"Who was?"

"Philip. Philip Otway. The man she's engaged to now."

"So you know him, too?" Her guardian looked at her curiously, with no trace now of the half-teasing smile that had lightened his glance a few minutes ago.

"It's Philip whom I really know," she explained with an effort. "He and his mother lived near my home. They were very kind to me during my father's lifetime. Then I found they—he was living in Paris, and that he was engaged to the girl who had—"

"Jilted me." He supplied the word with a sort of grim deliberation, and she nodded apologetically.

"But you strange girl, why make such a mystery of it?" He gave a slight annoyed laugh. "Why didn't you tell me?"

"I couldn't," she said simply. "You might have forbidden me to see him anymore, in view of the position between you and him."

"Oh, I see. And it was very important to you that you should see him again, Loraine?"

"Yes, very."

"Even though he was engaged to someone else?"

"That's difficult to explain, too. I didn't want—I didn't *intend*—to behave badly. But his mother insisted on telling me that Philip wasn't really madly in love with her—that, in fact, she, Elinor, had done most of the running."

"Interesting," he interjected dryly.

"I felt I couldn't bear just to let everything go by default. I wanted Philip to see me, not as the schoolgirl I had been, but as the girl I now am."

"Do you love him very much?" her guardian asked curtly.

"Yes, I love him very much," Loraine stated, softly but categorically. And at that, Paul got restlessly to his feet and walked up the room and back again.

As she watched him anxiously, she could not decide if he was very angry or deeply disquieted. She only knew that some quite powerful emotion prompted those restless steps and clouded his grimly handsome face. And after a moment she asked rather timidly, "Shall I go on?"

"Oh, Lord, yes! I suppose there's some more to tell."

"Quite a lot. But—but please don't stand over me like that while I'm telling it. You make me nervous."

He sat down again immediately, though without comment.

"I couldn't tell Philip about you, any more than I could tell you about Philip," she went on after a moment, and because her head was beginning to ache again, she pushed back her hair with a weary, absent little gesture. "I didn't *like* pretending to you both. In fact I hated it."

"I'm sure you did," he said brusquely. "It would have been so much simpler if you had confided in me from the beginning, Loraine."

"You weren't all that easy to confide in," she reminded him with a small pale smile. "Don't you remember?"

"I'm sorry. Go on."

"I hate to say it, but things were made much easier

for me when you went away. At least I didn't have to
practice any active deception or tell any downright lies.
But then Elinor discovered I was your ward.''

"How?" he asked briefly.

She explained about the telephone number, and he
smiled grimly and said, "Too bad. What did Elinor pro-
pose to do with that awkward information?"

Until that very moment Loraine had thought she
meant to tell Paul the whole story. But then she knew
suddenly that, however badly Elinor had behaved, she
simply could not betray her exact baseness to the man
who had once loved her and perhaps still did, in spite of
his anger.

She drew a long breath and said firmly, "I didn't
know that she proposed to do anything with it—until today. Then I was called to show some dresses to her, and
Philip and his mother were both there. I hardly know
how it happened, but some mention was made of where
I was living, and Elinor put it that I was living in your
flat, and—and Philip immediately jumped to some horrid conclusion—''

"What horrid conclusion?" Paul inquired with dry
exactness.

"The obvious one," she replied in much the same
tone.

"There is no obvious conclusion to draw except that
you are my ward," he said curtly.

"I meant, the obvious one when anyone uses that particular expression."

"You mean, in fact, that Elinor gave the statement a
particular and questionable flavor?"

"I was too stunned to notice just *how* she put it,"
Loraine lied gallantly. "I only knew that Philip was
appalled—''

"The censorious prig!"

"Oh, he *isn't*! Only, before I could straighten things
out, Madame Moisant came in and wh-whisked me off
to be photographed in the wedding dress and I was so
m-miserable I didn't know what to do," Loraine con-

fessed forlornly. And in spite of all she could do to prevent it, a lone tear trickled down her cheek and splashed onto the back of her hand.

"Don't cry," he said in a flat sort of voice. "I don't expect he's worth crying about. Few of us are."

"Oh, but he is!" She gulped and managed to choke back the rest of the tears. "He was always so wonderful to me. Like no one else at all. I know, in a way, he belongs to Elinor. But he belonged to me in a very special sense before he even met her."

"How?"

"It was when I was very much on my own because my father didn't really take much notice of me. And on my eighteenth birthday Philip found me, out on the moors, and he took me home to his mother and they gave me a heavenly, heavenly day I shall never forget. After that I used to see a lot of him."

"Did he ever make love to you?"

"No. I think he just thought of me as a schoolgirl, which I was then, of course," she added naively.

"But he doesn't think of you as a schoolgirl now?"

"I . . . don't think so."

"Not after seeing you in that wedding dress today," he said half to himself. "Florian's a clever devil."

Loraine opened her eyes wide and was on the point of asking how Paul could possibly know about the special significance of the wedding dress.

But at that moment he glanced at the clock and said, "Dear, have you noticed the time? I'm afraid your personal problems will have to wait for another day. Tomorrow isn't going to be much less strenuous than today, is it?"

"Oh, no! We have both the press show and the showing for the buyers." She smothered a yawn at the very thought and got to her feet. "I must go to bed. But I'm so glad I've told you, Paul."

"I'm glad, too." He also stood up, and as he looked down at her, she found his expression hard to fathom. It was indulgent, she was relieved to see, but there was a

curious touch of melancholy, too, in the way he looked
at her.

"Are you...disappointed in me?" she asked diffidently.

"Disappointed in you, child? No, of course not! Why
on earth should I be?"

"Well, I thought, you know, that it might seem to
you that I'd been deceitful and not—not at all like truth
itself, as you once said."

"You were not deceitful," he told her. "You were
just pushed against the wall and didn't know what on
earth to do next. If I had been half as understanding as I
should have been, you wouldn't have had to handle this
business alone."

"Oh, please don't blame yourself!" She put her
hands on his arms and looked up at him anxiously.
"There wasn't a thing you could have done about it,
even if you'd known more."

"No?" He took her face between his hands and
smiled down at her. "I wonder."

Then he kissed her, lightly but with an odd tenderness
that told her that any fault or indiscretion of hers was
entirely forgiven.

"Good night, Loraine. And try not to worry too
much. I know that sounds fatuous when one is miserable. But things have the strangest way of working out
in the end."

"Is that what you told yourself when *you* were
miserable?" she asked with a touch of mischief.

"No. If I had, I might have avoided a vital mistake,"
he replied dryly. "Now go to bed."

So she went to bed, though she would have liked to
linger and ask him just what he meant by that last admission. But it was too late now to go into the complications of his relationship with Elinor. She was sorry if he
felt he could have handled his own love affair better,
but she simply could not help thinking that, in point of
fact, he had had a lucky escape when Elinor had thrown
him over.

Incredibly, after all this emotional discussion, she slept dreamlessly and deeply and woke to a feeling of freshness and well-being.

True, the instinctive smile was wiped from her face when she recalled the scene yesterday in the fitting room. But with an illogical sense of comfort, she remembered Paul's saying that things had a strange way of working out in the end. And although she could not see her own affairs working out with any degree of satisfaction or simplicity in the near future, she recalled thankfully that at least she had taken her guardian into her confidence and would no longer have to guard every word and action while at home.

Once more he drove her down to the dress house, where she was greeted with cries of mingled congratulation and envy because she had captured most of the headlines in the morning newspapers.

It was the most extraordinary experience, to find oneself something of a minor celebrity and to see one's own face smiling back from the page of a newspaper.

"She has influence, that one," declared Lisette contemptuously. "Only so does one have one's photograph in the papers before the actual press show."

"No, no. She won the distinction on merit," countered Odette good-humoredly. "She was a sensation, the little Loraine. The biggest sensation since Gabrielle stole the show and married Monsieur Florian. Perhaps you also will marry romantically, *petite*."

"But not Monsieur Florian. She is a good little girl," mocked Lisette, "and does not take someone else's man. Is that not so, Loraine?"

"I hope so," said Loraine, but so soberly and thoughtfully that the other girls laughed, and Odette said it was as well not to commit oneself too far on such generalities.

The press show and the buyers' show lacked, perhaps, the drama of the opening day. About them there was no element of the theater premiere. But in practical fact, Loraine knew, they were at least as important. The one

supplied priceless advertisement and the other repre-
sented solid business.

Twice again she went through her part, not only to
the satisfaction of Florian, but in a manner that won her
the kind of notice and compliments she still found difficulty in accepting as hers. But she kept her head and
even contrived to remain pleasant and unruffled when
the representative of one of the more sensational papers
tried to extract intimate details of her private life from
her.

"You did well to say nothing so charmingly," Odette
told her with approval. "Now he will have to make it all
up."

"Make it up?" Loraine looked taken aback.

"To be sure. He will have his story, one way or
another. But now he will have the trouble of inventing
it."

"Oh," said Loraine, none too pleased. And for the
first time she glimpsed the kind of persecution that some
Continental newspapers turn upon the unfortunate
people classed as "newsworthy."

Again there was little time to think about her own affairs. But in the back of her mind there still hovered
both anxiety with regard to Philip and relief whenever
she thought about Paul.

In a way, I suppose I wasted yesterday evening, she
thought once. *I should have telephoned Philip and insisted on explaining the real position. Or at least I
should have got in touch with Mrs. Otway and asked her
advice. Instead....*

But how could she possibly regret what had happened
instead? Every time she thought of the way Paul had
looked after her, his understanding reception of her
confession and his particular method of reassurance,
she felt soothed and comforted.

All the same, she realized that she must somehow
contrive to give over this coming evening to the problem
of finding Philip and counteracting the mischief that
Elinor had done her. The longer she left things, the

worse they might well become. And it was significant
that Philip himself had not attempted to get in touch
with her.

True, he probably knew that she would have been
very late at the salon the previous night. But that not
even a telephone call had been received struck her now
as ominous. She grew more and more nervous and
anxious, therefore, as time went on and it was obvious
that another late evening was inevitable.

The last straw came when Marcelle—well-wishing but
dreadfully serious about everything—snatched a moment to run up from the boutique and inform her, ''A
very charming English *monsieur* is waiting outside for
you. But he has his car and he says it is all right. He will
wait until you can get away.''

''Oh, dear!'' Loraine exclaimed in dismay. She had
not expected Paul to repeat his good deed of the previous evening, and now it was going to be difficult to explain that he had waited in vain—that, in fact, all she
wanted was to go to Mrs. Otway's hotel and find out the
best way to get in contact with Philip.

''He is *very* charming,'' Marcelle repeated earnestly.

''Yes, I know.'' She could well imagine that the tall
distinguished Paul would appeal to Marcelle. ''But I wish
he wouldn't wait, just the same. Could you possibly—''

''He is not the kind to be put off,'' Marcelle declared
with considerable acumen. ''I would not wish to try,
Loraine. And now I must go.'' Which she did, with all
speed.

There was nothing else for it. Loraine just had to continue with her duties for another half hour, fretting all
the time over the knowledge that she would have to appear both ungrateful and obstinate when she did finally
join Paul.

She was free at last, however, and resolutely telling
herself that this time she must not be deflected from her
purpose, she ran downstairs and through the gay boutique, where Marcelle was painstakingly putting away
stock.

"He is still there," she said over her shoulder, but whether in congratulation or warning it was hard to say.

"I don't see him." Loraine gave a quick glance through the boutique window, but there was no sign of Paul's car anywhere.

"There—in the big gray Daimler right opposite the door." Marcelle left her work and came to stand beside Loraine and point out the car.

"*That* car? But Paul's car is— Oh!"

Suddenly the color flooded into Loraine's face and her heart began to beat fast and unevenly. For the man who was waiting in the gray Daimler was not Paul. It was Philip.

CHAPTER NINE

"PHILIP!"

Hardly waiting to call good-night to Marcelle, Loraine wrenched open the door of the boutique and ran out to the waiting car.

"Oh, Philip, how wonderful that you've come!" She bent down to greet him through the open window. "At least—" suddenly she remembered that he might have come in a mood of grim inquiry rather than friendly reconciliation, and her smile faded anxiously "—at least, I hope it is."

"Why shouldn't it be?" He smiled at her in the old way as he opened the door, and she felt her heart warm almost physically, as though it literally basked in the rays of that glorious moment. "Come on—I'm taking you to supper, and I'm not even listening to any excuses."

"You won't have to," she informed him happily as she slipped into the seat beside him. "Oh, Philip, what a lovely surprise!"

"But I sent up word that I'd be waiting for you. Didn't you get the message?" he inquired.

"Yes. But you were just described as a very charming English *monsieur*. I thought...."

"What did you think, with your long trail of admirers?" he wanted to know, but his tone was the half teasing, half affectionate one she loved.

"I thought it was Paul," she explained apologetically.

"I see." But there was no suggestion in his voice that the mention of Paul awoke either fury or dismay. "I trust I'm not a disappointment."

"No," she said simply. "I was so glad it was you that I even forgot you might still be angry with me."

"I was not angry with you at any time, Loraine," he informed her. And she thought there was a slight emphasis on the *you*, which suggested all sorts of interesting implications.

"Not after that dreadful scene in the fitting room, when Madame Moisant snatched me away before I could even explain my silly behavior?"

"I don't know quite what I felt then," he admitted, frowning even now at the recollection. "I was so bewildered and appalled and—yes, I was angry, I suppose. But then one tends to be angry when anything hurts a great deal."

"Oh, Philip, I'm so sorry. Did the discovery of my connection with Paul really hurt you?"

"No, darling. Not that. It was the feeling of being in some horrible mystery. And I thought at first— Well, it doesn't matter what I thought now, because it was idiotic of me ever to think of such a thing in connection with you," he declared. "But there are still a great many questions I want to ask."

"I'll answer them all willingly," she told him with a great sigh of relief. "It will be wonderful not to have any secrets anymore. I hope we're going somewhere quiet, where we can talk for ages."

"Leave that to me," he said, which she willingly did. And ten minutes later they were seated opposite each other at a corner table in a quiet, unpretentious little restaurant, where the checked cloths and the thick china did nothing to detract from the delicious food.

"Now—" he smiled at her as though the very sight of her made him contented "—the first question is why, for heaven's sake, did you think it necessary to conceal the fact that you were Paul Cardine's ward?"

"I thought you might not want to see any more of me if you knew."

"But, you absurd child, there was no *harm* in being his ward."

"No. But there could have been a great deal of embarrassment—both for him and for you. It wasn't that I thought you would blame me in any way. It was just that I thought you might decide it was all too difficult and that the best thing was to...drop me as gracefully as possible."

"You don't think much of me as a friend, do you?" He smiled reproachfully at her.

"I do, Philip, I do! But I couldn't help seeing how awkward the whole thing could be. Equally, I decided not to tell Paul, in case he forbade me to see you anymore."

"Would you have taken any notice if he had done such a thing?" he asked curiously.

"No. But it might have made things very awkward at home."

He laughed at that and said, "You're a darling," in the way he used to before Elinor had complicated the issue.

"So you trod your tightrope between us, deceiving both of us?" He laughed again, but this time with a note of admiration in his voice.

"I didn't like deceiving either of you," she said quickly, as she had to Paul. But, unlike her guardian, he grinned skeptically and said, "I bet you did! Girls always love a bit of mystery."

"I hated it!" she told him almost passionately. "And in the end I don't think it served me particularly well, for I had to make excuses not to see you, for fear you should find out."

"How did you think I might find out, Loraine?"

"The way you did in the end. By Elinor connecting Paul's telephone number with me."

He looked at her curiously and said, "How long had Elinor known about the telephone number?"

"I...don't know." She dropped her eyes, for, once more, she felt she could not be the one to expose Elinor's shabby behavior. "You'd better ask her about that, Philip."

"I can't very well."

"You mean it's difficult to discuss the whole thing with her?"

"No. I mean it's virtually impossible to discuss anything with her," Philip said calmly, "since we broke off our engagement this afternoon."

"Oh!" She glanced up quickly and then down again. And because convention has a curious compulsion upon all of us, she added, "I'm sorry," and then: "Was it about this unhappy business?"

"Not entirely. I don't think we were very well suited anyway, Loraine."

"Perhaps not." She glanced up again, and it struck her, for the first time, that under all that charm and ease of manner, Philip could be curiously hard.

It was not that he looked angry. He merely looked coldly indifferent, as though he had closed a book that had failed to interest him after all.

There was quite a long silence. Then she said with a rather nervous little laugh, "I find it hard to believe that everything has changed so much since Madame Moisant hurried me from the scene. I imagined I should find the greatest difficulty in explaining my motives—my behavior—to you. I left you looking angry and stunned, and hardly more than twenty-four hours later, you arrive outside the salon, smiling and full of understanding. Almost as though someone had forestalled me, and told the tale better than I could tell it myself."

"Someone did forestall you, Loraine." He smiled slightly. "And yes, made a very good job of telling the story, I suppose."

"Someone?" She opened her eyes wide in astonishment. "Someone told you the real position? But how could anyone? Do you mean—" her admiration for Mrs. Otway's shrewdness suddenly bounded up "—do you mean that your mother worked it out and convinced you that—"

"No, not my mother, dear. Your guardian."

"*Paul?* You can't mean it! But he hates—" She put her hand to her lips.

"Yes, I suppose he does hate me," agreed Philip with an air of smiling reflection. "He certainly gave no impression of appreciating my special charm. But we were extremely polite and civilized to each other and—"

"How did you meet?" she interrupted incredulously.

"We didn't meet, if you mean a chance meeting. He rang me up and asked if he could come and see me this morning."

"He did that?" she said softly. "It must have been a real sacrifice of pride."

"How about my pride?" inquired Philip amusedly.

"You aren't proud in the way Paul is. And anyway, you weren't the injured party," Loraine retorted, and not until she saw Philip make a slight face did she realize how determinedly she was identifying herself with her guardian. "But it was nice of you to see him," she added quickly.

"I thought so, too," Philip agreed carelessly, and she found herself wondering if he had adopted that smiling, half-mocking air toward Paul. Her guardian would have loathed it, she supposed.

"So Paul made it his business to tell you the true situation." Again she spoke half to herself and, putting her elbows on the table, she cupped her chin in her hands and stared thoughtfully at Philip. "You see now why I defended him that time you told me he was a tough nut."

"I see that you might have felt some sort of family loyalty, as it were," he conceded with a smile. "I still see no reason to query the general estimate. He's not a soft character."

"Not *soft*! Of course not. But he's kind and imaginative and—and sensitive."

"I feel bound to say he didn't strike me that way," Philip said dryly.

"But don't you see that it was sensitive of him to realize my distress, and both kind and imaginative to go and put things right on my behalf?" she said earnestly.

"I see that you like to explain his action that way," Philip told her indulgently. "For my part, I'm more inclined to think he had other motives. Human perhaps, but not quite so pure and sensitive."

"I don't know what you mean." She was indignant because she felt that the undercurrent of mockery in Philip's voice was intended for Paul, toward whom she felt very tender and grateful at this moment.

"Don't you, my sweet? That's because you're a nice, kind, unsuspicious girl," he told her teasingly. "But I, being a worldly, rather cynical sort of chap, can't help thinking that probably your guardian saw a priceless opportunity to make trouble between me and Elinor. And if that was his idea—" Philip shrugged "—he succeeded."

"He wouldn't think along those lines at all!" Loraine declared angrily. "And anyway—"

She stopped, for suddenly it occurred to her how little she really knew of her guardian and his personal affairs. She did remember his saying, when he first referred to the crisis of his broken engagement, that he took a lot of convincing that he was beaten. Had he been waiting all this time, ready to seize the first advantage offered, still refusing to believe that he had lost Elinor irretrievably?

She found she disliked the idea intensely and she felt annoyed with Philip—as far as she *could* feel annoyed with him, that was to say—when he went on reflectively, "He always took the break with Elinor very badly. I suppose he's been waiting for a chance like this, and suddenly saw the possibility of driving a wedge between us if he could make me see her as intriguing against me and my friends."

"If he saw her as clearly as that, I don't know why he should hope to get her back himself," said Loraine shortly.

"Dear child! A man in love doesn't mind much if his girl plays a dirty trick on someone else," Philip assured her lightly.

"And you think that Paul is a man in love?"

"I have no doubt of it. I see no other reason why he should have done what he did."

"You don't think it a sufficient reason that he should worry about my peace of mind and want to put things right for me?"

"I don't think Paul Cardine ticks that way," Philip said with a smiling shake of his head. "Besides, he said something about an ulterior motive—"

"*What* ulterior motive?" she asked quickly.

"I didn't pay much attention, really," Philip confessed. "Only, when I thanked him—rather coldly and correctly, of course—for taking the trouble to clarify the situation, he said in that slightly offensive way of his that I needn't think it was for the sake of my blue eyes and that he had his own ulterior motive. Something of the sort."

"Oh," said Loraine very soberly. "Oh, I see. Do you think that he and Elinor will now . . . will now . . . ."

"Loraine dear, don't ask me to speculate on Elinor's future," he begged with a slight grimace. "Still less on the future of Paul Cardine. I'm bound to say that the thought of both of them leaves me strangely cold just now."

"Oh, yes, I do understand!" She reached out her hand and lightly covered his as it lay on the table. "Forgive me for being so tactless. You can't be feeling very happy tonight, however much you may tell yourself that your engagement was a mistake."

"Funny you should say that." He turned his hand slowly and clasped hers. "As a matter of fact, I was just thinking how oddly happy I do feel, and that it was not quite decent of me to be so contented, in the circumstances."

She laughed softly at that and allowed her hand to remain in his for some seconds before she drew it gently away.

"Philip, dear, I ought to be going. It's been wonderful to have this long talk with you, and I've enjoyed my delicious supper all the more for being with you. But life is very hectic just now at Florian's and I shall feel dead tomorrow unless I get a good night's sleep.''

Unlike her guardian, he tried to persuade her to stay up a little longer. But she not only knew her own physical limitations, she sensed unerringly that the moment had come when he should be left to some quiet reflection. She had no wish to rush him from one emotional crisis to another, with the possibility of his wondering subsequently if he had acted too much on impulse.

And so she insisted on their going. He yielded with a good grace in the end and drove her home. But he kissed her with less than his customary lightness when he bade her good-night.

"When do I see you again?" he asked, holding her hand tightly so that she could not escape.

"Soon, soon," she promised blithely. "I'll ring you up when life is less demanding. Or you can ring me now."

"At Paul Cardine's number?" He laughed and made a face. But he let her go then, and she ran into the house, laughing a little to herself at the entrancing way life had changed since she had left the place that morning.

When she entered the flat she saw immediately that there was a light in the drawing room, and she guessed that Paul was, if not waiting for her, at least mildly curious about what she had been doing.

It was difficult not to feel a trifle self-conscious as she went in, but she managed to say quite casually, "Hello. So you're still up." ·

"It's not late for guardians," he told her a little disagreeably, "only for overworked wards. Where have *you* been all this time?"

"I went out to supper—with Philip."

"I see."

"Do you mind?"

"No."

She came and stood beside his chair. But he flicked over the pages of his book and gave the impression of paying scant attention to her—an attitude that both amused and annoyed her.

She could not have said quite what moved her to do so, but without saying anything she bent down and kissed his cheek.

Immediately he stopped turning the pages of his book and asked dryly, "What's that for?"

"You know perfectly well! And there's no need to be ashamed of your good deeds."

He laughed then and turned his head to look at her. But he said, "I'm not aware of having performed any especially good deeds today."

"Didn't you go to Philip—which you must have absolutely hated doing—and straighten out my affairs for me?"

"Part of my duties as a guardian," he told her. "You were too much occupied to attend to the matter yourself. But I wouldn't have anyone—not even a smug ass like Philip Otway—thinking you were living here in some sort of questionable relationship with me."

"You do have a graceful way of putting things, don't you?" she said crossly because she resented his description of Philip, even while she knew it was unreasonable of her to expect either man to do the other justice.

"I expect I'm in a bad temper," he replied with an extraordinarily disarming smile. "I'm sorry."

"It doesn't matter." She rubbed her hand up and down his arm in a reassuring little gesture. "Shall I tell you something that will put you in a good temper?"

"If you like." He smiled at her indulgently.

"Well...." She was slightly scared now she had come to the moment, and she could find no very delicate way of conveying the information. "Philip and Elinor have broken off their engagement."

This time, she noticed, not only his hand but every bit of him seemed to become absolutely still. Then he said,

"You think that's something to put me in a good temper?"

"At least it was something you very much wanted to happen, wasn't it?" she countered quickly, and found that she was holding her breath for his answer.

"Yes," he said slowly, "it was something I wanted more than anything else in the world."

He made the statement completely without emphasis, but she guessed that he was having some difficulty in controlling his feelings at that moment. She wished that she herself could have felt more enthusiastic about the whole thing. But, rather naturally, the thought of Elinor in connection with *anyone* close to her was unacceptable.

However, whatever the ulterior motive, her guardian had certainly bestirred himself well on her behalf, and it was only right that she should now show some friendly interest in his affairs.

"I gather they just decided that the engagement had been a mistake," she explained carefully.

But her guardian merely said dryly, "Very interesting." So she decided not to pursue the matter further and bade him good-night at this point and went to bed.

For no reason she could define she felt faintly depressed—perhaps as a reaction from all the emotional excitement of the evening. But then she remembered that everything was all right with Philip once more and that the future beckoned brightly. And on that happy reflection, she fell asleep.

Loraine had rather expected that, once the important first displays of the collection were over, life would become a trifle less demanding. But nothing could have been further from the case.

As a result of the fantastic success, yet again, of the Florian collection, customers crowded the salon daily. And in addition to the showing of the full collection, which took place every afternoon, there was endless work in connection with individual customers.

From Madame Moisant's brusque but satisfied manner and, still more, from the occasional Olympian nod she received from Florian, Loraine gathered that she was fulfilling her role with credit. But she still regarded herself very much as the new girl and did not expect to be chosen for any of the big social or charity events where Florian models went on unofficial display, as it were.

She was all the more flattered and pleased, therefore, when Florian summoned her one morning and said, "Loraine, I think it is time we used you for an outside assignment. In your naive way, you have become to a certain extent fashion news. You dance, I take it?"

"Yes, certainly, *monsieur*."

"I remember now, you said something about some ballet training, though this will not be necessary. At least—" he looked at her as though a new and pleasing thought had struck him "—one might use you for a minuet, I suppose. Could you learn that if necessary?"

She laughed. "I could dance a minuet when I was fourteen, *monsieur*. One does not forget anything so lovely in so short a time."

"True," he agreed with some approval. "How would you like to go to the Fête du Roi Soleil on the first of next month?"

"Monsieur Florian! It's the event of the season almost, isn't it?" She was breathless with excitement and delight.

"One could call it that, I suppose. It is not often that a new theater is opened in Paris, and this will celebrate the opening of the Monique."

"It's also a tremendous charity affair, isn't it?"

"Of course. Everything on which one spends a great deal of money is termed a charity affair," Florian agreed cynically. "And sometimes charity even benefits thereby."

"Monsieur Florian, I should adore to go! Please tell me some more," Loraine begged. And her youthful enthusiasm was so infectious that the great designer smiled indulgently, and, leaning back in his chair, looked more relaxed than she had seen him look since the new collection opened.

"Well, as the title implies, the actual stage spectacle will be cast in the mold of the seventeenth and eighteenth centuries," Florian explained. "That does not concern us. That is something for the theater world. But when the performance is over, there will be a ball—"

"On stage?" interjected Loraine eagerly.

"On the stage," Florian assured her. "Possibly this will include set, period dances with picked dancers—and there we might include you, *chérie*—though that I will decide later. In general, all you do is attend the fête wearing a Florian design, which will attract a certain amount of attention," he added without false modesty. "And so that no one shall give the credit to any of my rivals, you will be in my party."

"Oh, *monsieur*, how lovely!" Her eyes sparkled. "Who else will be there?"

"My wife, of course. Possibly Marianne and Roger Senloe, as they may be in Paris at that time. And—" again that indulgent smile "—I have no doubt you would like to choose your own partner for the occasion."

"You mean I can bring someone else?"

"Of course."

"They—he wouldn't have to wear fancy dress, would he?" She could not quite see Philip submitting to satins and laces.

"Oh, no!" Florian's expression suggested that he had no intention of submitting, either. "But in compliment to the event, your dress and my wife's dress will naturally have some suggestion of the period. A fascinating possibility," he murmured, half to himself, and already she could see him penciling absently on the block in front of him.

"Monsieur Florian, I think it's the most wonderful idea," Loraine told him. "And I can't thank you enough for choosing me. It *was* kind of you."

"It was also good judgment on my part, *chérie*," he

replied as he went on sketching. "You are the one I can see in a dress reminiscent of the period."

But he was smiling, she noticed, and she guessed he was not displeased to give her this treat—which was handsome of him, she reflected, when she remembered the scene of insubordination that had taken place in this very room on the morning of the opening day.

"Monsieur Florian," Loraine said on impulse, "I never really thanked you for the very kind way you helped me on the opening day of the collection."

"I do not recall, Loraine, that you left me much choice," he retorted with some humor.

"Oh, I know. I'm terribly sorry. But I thought you might like to know, *monsieur*, that—" she hesitated for the right words and compromised with a safe generality "—that everything is all right now."

"You are indeed fortunate, *petite*. I congratulate you," Florian said a little sardonically. "It is seldom that *everything* is all right with any of us. Pray tell me just what happened."

"Oh, well...." She had not quite bargained for a detailed statement, and now slightly regretted the impulse to express her gratitude by making this artless confidence. "You remember you were kind enough to promise me a very personal success when I wore the wedding dress?"

"What I said was that every man present would see in you the perfect, the inevitable bride," he corrected her firmly.

She laughed a little self-consciously.

"I thought you might like to know that the wedding dress had what might be called the right effect on the right person."

"You are remarkably cautious in your statements, *ma chère*." Florian was still sketching. "May I be indiscreet enough to ask you who the right person was?"

"I think you know. You saw him at the theater."

"Monsieur Philippe?" Florian looked up suddenly and straight across at her. "So you thought I was interested in the effect of the wedding dress on Monsieur Philippe?''

"I—you were kind enough to imply something of the kind."

"You are mistaken, *chérie*," he said, but quite gently. "Monsieur Philippe did not enter into my calculations, except as a minor counterplayer. The man whose reactions interested me profoundly was your guardian."

CHAPTER TEN

"My GUARDIAN, Monsieur Florian?" repeated Loraine in astonishment. "Why should you be interested in the way *he* reacted when he saw me in the wedding dress?"

"You didn't find his reactions interesting?"

"Well..." she began. Then she stopped. For with extraordinary poignancy she recaptured the moment when Paul had risen to his feet and murmured, "You darling!" as she passed. And she remembered how, inexplicably, this had brought tears into her eyes.

"I was very...gratified, of course, by his pleasure and admiration," she said at last.

"Gratified?" Florian made a disparaging little grimace. "Gratification is not a warm or an endearing emotion, Loraine. My impression was that you were greatly moved."

"Well, yes, I was," she admitted reluctantly.

"By the occasion, or by the unexpected tribute?"

"By both, I suppose," Loraine said slowly. "It wasn't at all what I had expected."

"No? I remember—" Florian reflectively penciled in a few extra lines on his sketch "—you said something very odd to me afterward in the dressing room. You said, 'I didn't look at Philip, after all. I looked at Paul.' Perhaps that also was unexpected?"

Loraine looked faintly startled and began to explain eagerly.

But Florian glanced suddenly at his watch and exclaimed, "You must go, *ma chère*, or you will be late for the afternoon show, and then Madame Moisant will be very angry with me as well as you."

There was no question of lingering after that to explain her reactions at length. He had already been generous with his time. So Loraine thanked him once more for his invitation to the Fête du Roi Soleil, and made her way down to the dressing room in a somewhat thoughtful state of mind.

"Well?" Madame Moisant greeted her with a mixture of sharpness and indulgence. "It was interesting, what Monsieur Florian had to say?"

"Yes, indeed, *madame*! Did you know that he had chosen me to go to the big fête at the Monique in three weeks' time?"

"Of course." Madame Moisant smiled with faintly acid amusement at the idea of her not knowing everything that went on under the roof of Florian's. "It was I who spoke up for you when we were discussing who would be suitable."

"Oh, *madame*, you darling!"

In her exuberant delight, Loraine flung her arms around the astonished *directrice* and hugged her—a tribute that had probably never before been paid to Madame Moisant.

"Come, come, Loraine, we will not be sentimental about it," she said, though in a tone of great good humor. "All is business in these matters. You were the most suitable and I said so. *Voilà tout!*"

"As you like." Loraine smiled almost affectionately at Madame Moisant. And then they were both caught up in the demands of the afternoon show and no more conversation was possible.

Not until Loraine was on her way home did she have much time to reflect on her conversation with Florian. And even then she naturally thought more of the exciting assignment for which he had chosen her than his odd insistence on the fact that Paul's reactions to the wedding dress had been of anything more than passing interest.

It was a pity I didn't have time to explain that Paul is too much in love with Elinor to have interesting reactions about anyone else, she thought amusedly. *Particularly now she's no longer engaged to Philip.*

Even so, Florian's words came back to her with some force when she entered the flat and found Paul, who had apparently preceded her by minutes only, standing by the hall table, turning over the one or two letters there.

He *had* been sweet about the wedding dress, and, in fresh gratitude for his affectionate admiration on that great occasion, she went over and put her arm around him.

"Hello, Paul!"

"Hello, my dear." He put down the letters and gave her a light guardianly kiss. "You're home early, aren't you?"

"For present time, yes. I don't know if I was just lucky or whether we're beginning to revert to normal."

"Time things were a little easier," he declared with some emphasis. "Florian's a slave driver. He's been working you to death."

She thought of telling him that Florian had spoken up well for him that afternoon and that he might display a little respectful gratitude. But suddenly she felt that, for some reason, the joke might fall a trifle flat. And so she just said something general about having to pay some sort of penalty for success.

"Very likely. But since you have an early evening for once, let's have a drink and then go out somewhere for dinner," he suggested. "It's too lovely an evening to stay in. I know a charming place about eight or ten miles along the river. What do you say?"

"That's an inspiration!" Loraine declared. "Just wait while I change and we'll go."

She ran to her room and quickly changed into the simple but infinitely becoming dress that Paul had once mistaken for a Florian model. And by the time she rejoined him in the drawing room, he had already poured out a glass of her favorite sherry.

Over their drinks she began to tell him about Florian's decision to include her in his party for the famous fête at the Monique. And then, in the middle of her description of her interview, Mimi came in to say that she was wanted on the telephone.

"Tell whoever it is not to keep you too long," Paul called after her, "or the best of the evening will be gone."

Loraine took care not to answer that specifically because she knew it was extremely possible that her caller was Philip. And sure enough, as soon as she lifted the receiver she heard that well-pitched, attractive voice that always made him sound as though he were smiling slightly.

"Darling Loraine! It's my lucky evening, I see. I hardly dared hope to find you in yet."

"We weren't quite so madly busy today, and I got away at something more like my usual time."

"Good for you. Let's celebrate the fact by going out somewhere together. I'll come and collect you in fifteen minutes, and meanwhile, you think out just where you'd like to go."

"Oh, Philip, I'm terribly sorry." She slightly lowered her voice, although, with the drawing-room door shut, Paul could certainly not hear what she was saying. "I'm afraid I can't."

"Why not?" he wanted to know.

"I've just arranged to go out with Paul."

"Can't you cancel that?"

"Well, no."

"Do you mean it's a long-standing arrangement, or just a spur-of-the-moment idea?"

"We both thought it was such a lovely evening, and as I was home early—"

"But *I* find it a lovely evening, too," Philip interrupted on a note of imperious good humor, "and I also would like to take advantage of the fact that you're home early."

"But, Philip, he asked me first."

"Good Lord, just explain to him that you have a more acceptable offer. A guardian isn't much more than a fill-in in one's social life, surely?"

"That's not at all the way I regard Paul," she said indignantly. "I couldn't think of saying such a thing to him."

"No?" Philip sounded amused but also slightly irritated by what he evidently regarded as excessive consideration for Paul's feelings. "Well, then, tell him you forgot you had a prior engagement with me, and that I've just rung up to remind you of the fact."

"But that isn't true."

"Don't be a darling little prig. It wouldn't be the first fib you've told him," was the laughing retort.

"I don't know what you mean by that, exactly."

"Only that you couldn't have skated over all the thin ice of the past few weeks without telling him a few lies," was the careless reply.

"I didn't tell him any lies! I only—"

"Well, don't let's split hairs about that now, sweetheart." This time there was an unmistakably impatient note in Philip's voice. "Tell him whatever your imagination and your conscience will permit, and be ready for me in a quarter of an hour."

"I'm sorry. I can't." For the first time in her life she felt a little spurt of genuine anger where Philip was concerned. "I've told you. I can't alter my present arrangement."

There was a very slight pause, during which she wondered apprehensively if she had made him really angry in his turn. But perhaps he had heard the unusual note in her voice. At any rate, when his reply came it was not at all what she expected. He said gently and persuasively, "Loraine, dear, I've something very important to say to you. Can you really not find time for me?"

"Oh, Philip, *any*time but tonight! You have no idea how sorry I am to say no. But—" she lowered her voice still further "—it would be a sort of slap in the face to Paul."

"I could bear that," he replied callously.

"Well, I couldn't," stated Loraine flatly. And then,

as though to soften that: "The very next early evening I can manage—"

"That might be too late." His voice was unbelievably a trifle cold. "I'm going back to England soon."

"Going back to England!" She was aghast. "But you *can't.* I was just going to tell you— Florian wants me to join his party for the fête at the Monique, and he said I could bring my own partner, and of course I want to have *you.*"

He laughed at that. A much more indulgent, Philip-like laugh. But he said teasingly, "Why don't you take your guardian, if he's so important to you?"

"Because I want you," she said simply.

"Darling Loraine!" He laughed again, and this time sounded exactly like his old self. "Well, I'll forgive you for this evening's defection, then, and tell you I shan't be longer than a week in England. So I shall be back in time for the fête."

"I'm so—glad." She actually gulped in her relief. "But I'd like to see you before you go, if possible. Can't we manage anything, Philip?"

"When will you be finished tomorrow?"

"I don't know," she admitted. "But I'll try my very, very best to get off early."

"All right. I'll fetch you from the salon. Phone me when you look like being free, and I'll come along."

"Oh, thank you! And I'm terribly sorry about this evening. But I must fly now!" She glanced at her watch, realized that they must have been talking far longer than Paul would consider reasonable, and hastily rang off before he could engage her in further conversation.

"I'm sorry. . . ." She came back breathlessly into the drawing room, feeling this was certainly her evening for being apologetic. "I'm afraid I've been rather a long time."

"That's all right. Who was your loquacious caller?" her guardian wanted to know.

"Philip."

"Oh?" Paul raised disparaging eyebrows. "What did *he* want?"

"To take me out for the evening," retorted Loraine, who thought he deserved that for his way of referring to Philip.

"Well, why didn't you go?" was the slightly disagreeable inquiry.

"Because I had a previous engagement."

"Oh, Loraine," he laughed, and his face cleared so that he looked almost boyish instead of slightly forbidding. "You're a sweet child." He put out a hand and drew her down onto the arm of his chair. "I don't know what I ever did to deserve to have you for a ward."

"Nothing at all," she reminded him, though with a quick and mischievous smile. "I should think my father just took a list of the less remote relations and stuck a pin in it."

"And I was the one who got stabbed," he said reflectively. "It's a sobering thought."

"Shall we go?" she laughed. But she suddenly felt overwhelmingly glad that she had resisted all Philip's arguments and blandishments. It would have been horrible to make some thin and obvious excuse, and then to go off and leave Paul alone. Rather the sort of thing Elinor might do.

And then she wondered how far he had got—if at all—with straightening out his affairs in that direction. And she decided to ask him when the right moment arose.

As they drove out of Paris and along the Seine they talked very little. It was enough just to enjoy the soft evening air that blew in through the open window of the car, to delight in the beauty of the scene around them and, if the truth be told, remain content in each other's company.

That was the remarkable thing, Loraine thought idly once. Nowadays she was so completely relaxed and at ease in her guardian's presence that it was difficult even to recall how inhibited and unhappy she had once felt.

The place he had chosen was practically on the river bank, and presently they were installed at a table on the terrace, overlooking the broad smooth stretch of the Seine.

"It's heavenly, Paul," she said with a sigh of contentment. "Have you been here often?"

"Often enough to know that I like it on a summer's evening after a strenuous day."

"Did you come here with Elinor?" she inquired on impulse.

"Once or twice." He studied the menu with attention.

"And you might do so again, I suppose?"

"One never knows."

She laughed, a little piqued. For, after all, he knew enough about *her* private affairs. She was only showing a friendly reciprocal interest.

"I suppose that rather cagey air means that I mustn't ask any more questions?"

"No. It means that I don't know the answers yet to the kind of question you probably want to ask me."

"Oh, I'm sorry."

She was. Genuinely sorry. For she realized that, however much the breaking of Elinor's engagement might have raised his hopes, the fact was that he was probably still a long way from reestablishing his own position with her.

"That's all right." He looked up and grinned at her across the table. "Shall we talk about something else?"

"Yes, of course," she agreed quickly. And presently she reverted to the conversation that Philip's telephone call had interrupted, and began to explain in detail Florian's plans in connection with the Fête du Roi Soleil.

"So Florian wants you to bring a partner." He looked reflective. "Who is it going to be?"

"Why, Philip, of course." Then, because she thought he might find that a bit naive, she hurried on. "He has to go to England for a week or so—they have property there, you know—but fortunately he will be back in good time.''

''Very fortunate,'' agreed Paul, so dryly that she felt a momentary flicker of annoyance. But then she reminded herself yet again that it was asking too much that two men who had been rivals over the same girl should think particularly well of each other.

''You don't mind my going with Philip, do you?'' she asked a little anxiously.

''I have nothing against him from a guardian's point of view, Loraine. But—'' Paul smiled wryly ''—you mustn't expect me to go as far as liking him personally.''

''I don't,'' she said earnestly. ''And I think it's extraordinarily good and tolerant of you, in the circumstances, not to oppose my friendship with him.''

''I haven't much choice in the matter,'' he replied curtly. ''You told me you loved him, and I want your happiness.''

''I know you do.'' She put out her hand and touched his, lightly and gratefully.

But perhaps he thought that was overdoing the emotional side of things somewhat, because he drew his hand away quite decidedly and said, ''To study his ward's happiness is the proper attitude for a guardian, I take it.''

''Well,'' she said with a laugh, ''for a nice guardian, yes. Anyway, I appreciate the attitude, Paul. And I only hope your own affairs smooth out as completely as mine have done.''

He looked at her curiously.

''Just how far *have* your affairs smoothed out, Loraine?'' he asked suddenly. ''You've never told me, categorically, you know.''

''But I don't have to surely?'' She opened her eyes. ''You know better than anyone else. It was you who explained everything to Philip. And now he knows everything; I'm happy.''

''But that surely isn't the height of your ambition as far as Philip Otway is concerned?''

"Well, no." She laughed and colored as she glanced down at the tablecloth and traced the pattern on it with a deliberate forefinger. "It's naturally as important to me as to you that he broke off his engagement with Elinor. But now, oddly enough, you and I are in rather the same position. We just have to wait for the next stage. One can't hurry these things. I know Philip loves me—"

"How do you know?"

"It's in everything he does and says! The way he looks at me, speaks to me, smiles at me...."

"I see."

"When you love someone, you don't need to be told everything in words of one syllable, do you?"

"No, Loraine, I suppose not," he agreed gently. Then he made an odd little movement of his shoulders and said, "Shall we go now? It's getting late and a bit chilly."

She realized then that the soft mellow charm of the evening had faded, and there was a curious unseasonable touch of bleakness about the night that had fallen.

"Yes, let's go," she agreed quickly. And she was glad that, on the way back, he put up the window and showed little disposition to talk further. Presently she fell asleep against his shoulder and woke only when they drew up outside their home.

The next morning, at breakfast, he told her he would be out that evening, which made it easy for her to explain that she also would not be home, as Philip was meeting her from work.

"Very well. Don't make too late a night of it," Paul said in his most guardianly way.

"No, sir," Loraine promised, dropping a submissive little curtsy, for which she got her ear pinched. But he kissed her, too, before she went off, and she felt the day had started on an auspicious note.

To deepen the impression, she found Madame Moisant in an exceptionally good and indulgent humor, and throughout the day customers seemed singularly easy to

please. Even Lisette was less provocative and tiresome
than usual. Feeling that this must be her lucky day,
Loraine decided that her meeting with Philip could only
be a radiant success.

All the same she breathed a sigh of relief when she
finally came out, to find him standing there beside his
car, smoking a cigarette and looking handsome enough
to make most women look at him twice.

"If you're not careful, you'll be mistaken for a star
model yourself and be photographed for one of the
glossy magazines before you know where you are," she
warned him as she came up.

"Heaven forbid!" he said in his most British way.
"Though now you're here, no self-respecting photog-
rapher would think of taking anyone else. How lovely
you're looking, my sweet child."

"Part of the Florian treatment," she assured him
lightly.

But he said, "Nothing of the sort. Sheer natural
Loraine charm. I should know. I've seen it develop
from the schoolgirl stage."

"Oh, Philip—" she laughed reminiscently as she got
into the car beside him "—that seems such a long time
ago!"

"What does, dear?"

"The day you first found me, sitting on the ground
and moping, because it was my eighteenth birthday and
no one knew or cared. And you took me home to your
mother and gave me a wonderful birthday."

He laughed, too, on a note of pleasant recollection.

"Well, I'm going to do much the same thing now—
take you home to my mother. But only for half an hour.
She says she hasn't seen you for ages, and I promised we
would call in and have a drink with her before going out
on our own."

"Lovely," said Loraine—but mostly for the specific
reassurance that she and Philip were going to be on their
own for most of the evening.

All the same, it was pleasant to see Mrs. Otway and

receive fresh praise for her triumph on the opening day
of the collection. She hardly even minded when Mrs.
Otway found an excuse for sending Philip off on some
errand for her, which gave them ten minutes alone
together, though she did feel faintly uncomfortable
when her hostess plunged immediately into the delicate
subject of the broken engagement.

"I'm *so* relieved and satisfied to have seen the back
of Elinor Roye," Mrs. Otway stated with brevity and
candor. "And quite grateful to you, dear, for the little
part you played in bringing Philip to his senses."

"Well, I don't know that I did anything very active—" Loraine began.

"No, no," Mrs. Otway agreed just a trifle too em-
phatically. "I wouldn't want to make you feel you were
seriously involved. It was just that, at that exact moment, he needed reminding that there were plenty of
other attractive girls around besides the one he had,
most mistakenly, chosen. You provided just that reminder, darling, and I'll always remember you gratefully for that."

"Th-thank you," said Loraine uncertainly, for she
could not escape the curious impression that she was
being relegated, charmingly and affectionately, to the
past.

"You and I, who know our Philip so well," went on
Mrs. Otway, smiling, "can afford to be indulgent over
the fact that he is a tiny bit too susceptible. But I must
say we organized a lucky escape for him that time,
didn't we?"

Mrs. Otway laughed reminiscently. But Loraine did
not laugh, either reminiscently or otherwise. She stared
at her hostess in something between astonishment and
dismay, unable to decide if she were being given a firm
hint, or if Mrs. Otway genuinely did not realize the true
position.

It was not up to Loraine to disillusion her at this
point. But she thought of Philip saying that he had
something very special to tell her, and she almost wished

she could give the other woman some sort of hint of what was coming.

She won't really like me much more than Elinor in the role of Philip's wife, she thought with a sudden flash of insight. *She wouldn't like anyone as Philip's wife. But perhaps I can win her over gradually.* In her certainty and her inner happiness she could afford to feel generous.

But her degree of tolerance was sorely tried when Mrs. Otway went on, still in that smiling, reminiscent sort of way, "I've always thought of you as an affectionate younger sister for Philip, you know, Loraine dear, and I'm afraid I took it very much for granted that you would help me to save him from Elinor. If I was a bit crude about it, I know you will forgive me and understand."

She paused, and Loraine finally said, "Of course," because there was really nothing else to say unless she proposed to enter into some kind of argument, which was unthinkable.

"One of these days, you and I will be able to congratulate ourselves afresh when Philip *really* finds the right girl," the older women went on pleasantly, "and then we shall feel that all the trouble over Elinor was well worthwhile. It's a sort of—what shall I say—family solidarity, isn't it, darling?"

Fortunately Loraine was saved from having to give her views on this version of family solidarity, for at this moment Philip returned with the headache remedy that his mother had requested.

She now seemed, Loraine could not help observing, singularly bright for anyone with a headache, and she wondered if Philip also knew that he had been sent out of the way for a purpose.

Anyway, it doesn't matter, Loraine told herself almost passionately. *Nothing matters except that Philip and I are to be on our own at last, with no shadow between us. It isn't as though he doesn't know the situation. It was he who told me about her aversion to his marrying at all. But he's quite capable of managing her in the few things that matter to him, and we'll find a way—he and I—to reconcile her to our marriage.*

It was a relief, however, when they did get away on their own. For whatever excuses one might make for her, Mrs. Otway had really been quite insufferable, and no smiles or endearments could make up for the brutal clarity with which she had tried to brush off Loraine now that she had no further need of her.

Loraine had had it in mind to tell Philip—lightly, amusingly—of his mother's efforts. But when it came to the point she found she could not, and they talked of other things.

"I'm taking you to the Corbeille des Fleurs," Philip told her. "Do you know it?"

"No." She shook her head. "But it sounds attractive."

"I like it. We have to drive some way, but it's worth it when one gets there," he assured her. And so happy was she to be driving in his company and talking without the necessity of guarding her words, that she hardly noticed where they were going, and it was some while before the suspicion came to her that they were heading for the place to which Paul had taken her the previous evening.

The discovery disconcerted her beyond measure—as though, in some subtle way, she were being disloyal to her guardian. They had enjoyed themselves so much there, discussed their most intimate affairs there, and in some curious sense made the place very much their own.

Now the idea that she was going there with Philip—probably to receive his proposal—made her so uncomfortable that she almost asked him to turn back and drive her somewhere else.

The impossibility of this, however, became immediately plain to her. Probably Philip had arranged this evening in some detail. It was not for her to spoil it by informing him that she already associated his chosen venue with someone also very dear to her—though in an entirely different way, of course.

Her dismay was complete when they were even shown to the same table—Paul's table—and she simply had to invent some mild complaint about too much breeze and have another table found for them. And then, just as she began to hope she could keep her strange distress within bounds if she sat with her back to that charming familiar corner, up came the same waiter who had waited on Paul and her, and, smiling at her in a fatherly way, he observed that it was pleasant to see *mademoiselle* back so soon.

"Have you been here before, then?" Philip glanced at her quickly. "I thought you said you didn't know it."

"I didn't know the name. I recognized it, of course, when we got here."

"When did you come before?" he wanted to know, obviously a little disappointed that he was not providing a novelty, after all.

"Last night," Loraine said reluctantly.

"Last night?" He was plainly both disgusted and put out. "With your guardian?"

"Yes."

"What an odd place for him to bring you."

"Oh, why, Philip? It's such a lovely place that I suppose it's one of the natural spots to think of if one wants to give pleasure," she said in an effort to mollify him.

He laughed shortly. She had never seen him quite so obviously annoyed and disconcerted.

"It's what I would describe as a romantic spot," he retorted. "I should have thought a mere guardian would have chosen something much more solid and conventional."

"There's nothing solid or conventional about Paul!"

"Are you telling me there's something romantic about him, then?" was the dry inquiry.

"Why, no," said Loraine, and immediately knew that was not correct. Her guardian was, in his way, what one meant by romantic, she supposed. Only she could not possibly define just what degree of romanticism was involved to a rather angry Philip. Instead she said in a placatory way, "Philip, you sound quite cross with me. I don't know why."

"I'm sorry." He laughed and, reaching over, patted her hand. "Only you're up in arms in a moment if there's so much as a hint of criticism where your guardian's concerned."

"Am I?" She considered that without rancor. "Well, I suppose I'm very fond of him."

"I suppose you must be," agreed Philip a little coolly, and he turned his attention to the menu.

It is always difficult to say what makes or spoils an atmosphere. Still less is it possible to command the magic that comes only from the fusing of thought and feeling between two people. One can make the most elaborate and careful preparations, entertain the highest hopes and yet, for some inexplicable reason, the incandescence never glows, the spirit never soars.

For a couple of hours Loraine and Philip sat opposite each other, talking, laughing, recalling past occasions together. Outwardly they were a charming couple, enjoying each other's company exceedingly. But in her heart, Loraine knew that something had gone wrong. The minutes ticked by, and never once did Philip mention the very special "something" he had wanted to tell her.

CHAPTER ELEVEN

LORAINE TRIED TO TELL HERSELF that on the way home it would be different. They would be entirely alone, in the seclusion of the car, and probably *that* was when he planned to tell her what was in his heart.

But when it came to the return journey he drove rather fast, and they talked of quite trivial things, so that it was impossible for her even to refer lightly to the fact that he had said he had something special to tell her—and what was it?

As they neared home, the only thing of importance that she could bring herself to ask was, "When do you go to England, Philip?"

"I'm not quite sure, sweetheart." He still used charming terms of endearment, so that from time to time she wondered if she had simply imagined the glass barrier between them, and if what she took for withdrawal was no more than the tactful timing of a man who had recently broken off a previous engagement.

"I expect it will be at the end of this week or the beginning of next," Philip said after a moment's reflection.

"But you'll be back in plenty of time for the fête?"

"That's a promise!" He gave her a quick reassuring smile that did a good deal toward compensating her for an evening that had certainly not fulfilled her bright hopes.

When they parted he kissed her—a longer, more significant kiss than any he had given her so far—and he said in his most endearing and beguiling way, "I'm sorry I was ill-tempered earlier in the evening."

"Oh, Philip, you weren't! Or, if you were, it doesn't matter now."

"My kind, forgiving little Loraine! But the fact is that I get jealous every time you grow starry-eyed about that wretched guardian of yours."

She ought of course, to have assured him he had no need to be jealous of anyone, or at least to repudiate laughingly any charge of being starry-eyed about Paul. But instead of following either of these wise courses, she simply said stubbornly, "He's not a wretched guardian. He's a dear and I'm very fond of him. I understand your not being able to do him justice, but please, Philip, don't run him down to me. I can't take it and I won't."

"Loyal Loraine," he said, but mockingly rather than approvingly. "But don't rely on him too much in the future, my sweet. When he gets back his Elinor—or she gets him back—you won't be the most welcome of guests in your guardian's household anymore."

For some reason or other she was so angry at that that she looked him coolly in the eye and remarked casually, "I might be married myself by then."

"True," he said, "you might." And putting two fingers under her chin, he tilted up her face and kissed her again. "You're sweet when you're angry."

Then he bade her good-night and drove away almost before she had had time to enter the building.

She felt depressed again. But she still felt angry. It was an odd experience, to feel really angry with Philip, for this carried with it something she had never exercised toward him before—a distinct suggestion of criticism.

He had no right to run down her guardian to her. And it had been horrid and slightly malicious of him to remind her of the unwelcome part that Elinor would probably play in any future life with her guardian. Most of all, when he had specifically said he had something special to tell her, he should have found some chance for doing so.

Perhaps I'm an optimistic fool, she thought as she

went up in the lift. *Perhaps I jumped to too hasty con-clusions. He might not have meant what I thought he meant. But then he must have meant something. And absolutely nothing of special interest was discussed—except perhaps his journey to England.*

The lift stopped at that moment, but she went on standing there, for the chill idea had come to her that perhaps *that* was all he had meant. She racked her brains to remember the exact sequence in his tele-phone conversation, and she was nearly sure that he had mentioned the important "something" at an early stage. He had advanced it as a pressing reason for her seeing him.

And then, when I held out against his arguments and suggested a later meeting, Loraine recalled reluctantly, *he said he would have to go home to England.*

Slowly she got out of the lift and fumbled for her key.

If that were the real explanation of what had once seemed a radiant statement, fraught with lovely sig-nificance, then indeed she had been deluding herself. But there was no denying it *was* a possible explanation.

"I've been a fool, just as I thought," Loraine told herself.

But even as she reproached herself, she remembered that it was Philip's very special air toward her that had first given her the idea that he might well be going to ask her to marry him.

The words to which she had pinned so much hope might not, it was true, have that exact significance at that exact time. But his whole attitude had justified her belief that one day he intended to say the words she longed to hear.

She entered the flat in a very sober mood. But then she saw, by the light in the drawing room, that her guar-dian must have already returned, and a sense of in-describable relief and pleasure swept over her. It was like finding that a bright fire was burning when one came into what one had expected to be an empty house on a cold night.

"Oh, Paul, hello!" She went in to greet him. "Did you get home early after all?"

"Only about twenty minutes ago." He smiled across at her indulgently, perhaps because her own pleasure was so patent. "Have you had a good time?"

"Lovely, thank you," she said a trifle too quickly.

"Where did you go?"

"Oddly enough, to the same place that you chose last night."

"Oh, no!" A look of annoyance and protest came into his face and, feeling that she simply could not bear to have a fresh argument, she cried, "Don't *you* be cross with me about it! A girl can't help it if two men happen to like the same restaurant."

"I'm not cross with you, Loraine," he said, and held out his hand to her.

With a little rush she came into the circle of his arm and leaned against him with a fresh sense of relief and reassurance.

"Who was cross with you, dear?" he asked gently.

"Well, Philip was rather." She didn't really want to tell him about Philip's fall from grace, but it was so wonderful to have a sympathetic confidant. "You see, I didn't know the name of the place—I don't think you mentioned it last night—and I didn't realize where we were going until we had almost arrived."

She stopped. But the silence was so subtly encouraging that she went on.

"It was too late to say anything or make any rearrangement."

"Did you want to, Loraine?" he asked mildly.

"Very much so!"

"Why, dear?"

"Well, I felt it was rather *our* place, you know. It had been such a lovely evening, just you and me together, and we'd talked about such very personal things. I didn't really want to associate the place with anyone else."

"Very sweet of you," he said, and touched her cheek,

smilingly, with gentle fingers. "However, as you say, it was too late to make any change when you discovered where you were going."

"Yes. And, as I thought Philip would be disappointed to find I had already been there, I said nothing. But then we had the same waiter, and he recognized me and said it was nice to see me again so soon."

"Extremely awkward," agreed Paul, biting his lip slightly but not entirely concealing his amusement.

"Of course, Philip asked me when I had last been there, and I had to tell him and he wasn't at all pleased."

"Too bad," said Paul cheerfully.

"It *was* too bad," she assured him a little reproachfully. "In some way I can't explain, it spoiled the evening."

"Do you mean he sulked?"

"Oh, no!" She could not allow that Philip had done anything so petty as that. "No, he didn't sulk. But—" she sighed involuntarily "—somehow the magic was gone."

"I'm so sorry," he said kindly, and lightly ruffled her hair. "But magic's a curious and elusive quality, Loraine. One can never arrange it or account for it. The only thing I can tell you is that, at your age, it does tend to recur."

"Dear Paul! You're so comforting." She hugged him. "Now tell me about your own evening. Did you go out with one of your colleagues?"

"No. I went out with Elinor."

"Oh." For some reason she felt an inexpressible chill—possibly at the sheer mention of Elinor, who had caused her so much heartache and might do so again. "And it was satisfactory?"

"Very satisfactory indeed."

"I'm so glad for you," Loraine said earnestly. But she thought of what Philip had said about her not being welcome in Paul's house once Elinor returned to the picture. And the prospect caused her such acute dismay that, in order to hide it, she had to pretend to give a slight yawn and said she must go to bed now.

He did not offer to detain her. So she slipped from the arm of his chair, where she had been sitting, dropped a light but dutiful kiss on the top of his head and turned to go.

But then, when she reached to door, she was overwhelmed by such an irresistible impulse to know more of the circumstance that would affect her so deeply that she turned back and looked at him across the room.

"Are you...are you going to be married quite soon, Paul?" she asked, unable, in her anxiety, to think of a way to soften the crudeness of that.

He raised his eyebrows.

"I have no idea, Loraine."

"You...you didn't get as far as discussing that with Elinor?"

"No. But why are you so anxious to know about my future plans?"

"Well, they do affect me, too, don't they? I mean, once you're married to Elinor I couldn't expect to be very welcome in your home and I should have to find—"

"There will never be a time when you're not welcome in my home, my dear," he interrupted firmly. "This *is* your home, until you yourself choose to go elsewhere."

"Oh, Paul." Suddenly she felt the tears rush into her eyes, just as they had when he paid that tribute to her in the wedding dress. No one—not even her father—had ever said categorically that she had a home that was hers beyond question or discussion, and the fact that her guardian chose to make her position so blessedly clear moved her beyond description.

It was true that Elinor might still make the situation impossible if she so chose. But with the feeling that nothing could ever, ever take away the warmth and tenderness of that simple declaration, Loraine ran back and dropped on her knees beside her guardian's chair.

"Oh, Paul, how dear of you to put it into words like that!"

"Darling child, there are certain basic things that need putting into words sometimes," he told her with a smile. "It's neither admirable nor kind to leave such things in any doubt." And leaning forward, he kissed her, lightly but reassuringly. As he did so, the most comforting conviction came to her that, in a sense, no one, not even Elinor, could ever really spoil the very special relationship that now existed between them.

This is the really important moment of the evening, she told herself as she got up and went slowly away to bed.

And if she decided later that this was a slight exaggeration, due to the understandable emotion of a touching occasion, at least the memory of it lingered pleasantly in the back of her mind.

During the next few days preparations for the Fête du Roi Soleil assumed a very important place in Loraine's life. It was evident that the combining of the period of the fête with the demands of an up-to-the-minute design presented a challenge to artistry and ingenuity that Florian immensely enjoyed.

As usual, he worked largely in silence. But from time to time—particularly when things went well and he felt genial—he would talk to Loraine, and then showed the liveliest curiosity about her personal arrangements.

"So Monsieur Philippe is happy to join us at the fête?" he said.

"Indeed, yes! He has to go to England on business in between," Loraine explained, "but he will return to Paris in good time."

"And if he does not?"

"If he doesn't what, *monsieur*?"

"Return in time."

"Oh, but he *will*!" Loraine was scandalized at the idea that Philip could possibly be thought capable of failing on such an occasion.

"The unexpected does happen sometimes," retorted Florian, somewhat captiously, she thought. "It is as well to make alternative arrangements. Perhaps your guardian would be willing to hold himself in readiness, in case of difficulty.''

"I couldn't possibly ask him to do that, Monsieur Florian!" She could imagine Paul's reaction at being asked to keep himself free as a possible stand-in for Philip. "And, in any case, I assure you it won't be necessary.''

"Famous last words," muttered Florian disagreeably, and Loraine found herself thinking that charming Madame Florian must sometimes have a difficult time of it. Though, one was bound to admit, she looked remarkably serene and happy most of the while on the Florian treatment.

Faintly annoyed though she was by Florian's expressed doubts, Loraine decided she would impress on Philip the absolute necessity of being back in good time. She would make a point of it when she saw him before his departure.

She was all the more put out, therefore, when he had to go at unexpectedly short notice and was only able to telephone to say goodbye.

"I'm desperately disappointed not to see you, Loraine dear," he said in that tone that made her momentarily forget everything else. "But if I make a point of being in London early tomorrow morning, there's a chance of my being included in one of the most important art shows of the season. You do understand, don't you?''

"But of course, Philip." She gallantly swallowed her disappointment. "As long as you're back in good time for the fête, it's perfectly all right. We'll make up for any present disappointment then.''

"Indeed we will," he promised. "Goodbye for the time being, my sweet. Here's mother to say a word to you, too.''

Mrs. Otway then came on the telephone and made her goodbyes in the most affectionate manner, but with a touch of finality that enabled Loraine to ask her quite innocently if she was not returning to Paris later.

"Oh, I don't think so, darling. After all, England *is* our home," she reminded Loraine with a slight and charming laugh. "We have to spend some time there."

"Of course," Loraine agreed, successfully concealing her relief and satisfaction at the thought that Mrs. Otway would not be on the scene at all when she next saw Philip. Then she repeated her goodbyes with polite cordiality, and rang off with the faintly guilty and not altogether welcome reflection: *Elinor must sometimes have felt exactly like this!*

She supposed, in consequence, that she might even try to feel a little more indulgent and well-wishing toward Elinor. But it was not possible—oddly enough, more because of her present connection with Paul than for past injuries, now half forgotten and forgiven.

Men are so silly. Even the dearest of them, thought Loraine in newfound wisdom. *Of course, it's entirely his own business, but I* wish *my darling, otherwise sensible guardian could see that Elinor isn't really the woman to make him, or any man, happy.*

She had, however, already interfered more than enough in the course of Elinor's love life, and she felt exaggeratedly anxious not to say or do anything even remotely unfair to her now. So she held her peace. But it depressed her so much even to think of Paul being deeply involved with Elinor once more that she tended to push the whole subject into the back of her mind and concentrate instead on the details of the coming fête.

This was not difficult for, by now, at the salon there was little talk of anything else. Whatever the jealousies and rivalries—and they were always legion—no one could ever resist taking some sort of part in anything that affected the prestige and success of Florian's.

Down to the smallest, most junior assistant in the workrooms, picking up pins, they were all gratified and interested because several Florian models would, in Madame Moisant's phrase, "be attending the fête," in addition to the fact that Loraine—and, as it turned out, Gabrielle Florian, too—were to be included in the exhibition minuet that would be danced during the evening.

"Though why *they* should be chosen one cannot imagine," Lisette remarked with a contemptuous little shrug. "Loraine is hardly more than a silly schoolgirl, while Madame Florian is almost a middle-aged married woman now. Thirty at least."

No one fell into the trap of trying to explain the choice to Lisette. And so she was reduced to sulky silence and some baleful reflection on the fact that the ideal age for those chosen would have been twenty-two, which was her own age exactly.

Inevitably Loraine saw a good deal of Gabrielle as well as her husband during this time, and she was touched and interested all over again to see the charming relationship between them.

"Yours must have been a real romance," she said once when, after a long evening fitting, she and Gabrielle were changing on their own in the models' dressing room.

"Oh, it was!" Gabrielle laughed reminiscently. "Being in this dressing room brings it all back so much. Though the odd thing was that, half the time I was here, I thought I was in love with someone else."

"Did you really?" Loraine looked interested. "But then Monsieur Florian convinced you otherwise?"

"Not exactly. I found it out for myself, and I thought he was indifferent to me. It was frightful!" she declared, but cheerfully, in view of the fact that it was all safely over so long ago. "*I* had to convince *him* in the end," she added reflectively.

"That he loved you?"

"Oh, no! Apparently he'd been doing that for some time, dear Georges!" said Gabrielle, thereby astonishing Loraine who, like most people, simply could not think of Florian by any name but the one that he had made so famous.

"He thought the other man was the obvious and suitable one, you know," Gabrielle explained, "and that he himself wasn't young enough for me and too worldly and all that. But it came out all right in the end. And the other man married someone else perfectly sweet, for which I was very glad.''

"Well, if you can speak of him like that, you must have got over him completely," Loraine said with a laugh.

"Oh, but, my dear, one does!" Gabrielle assured her. "At one moment you think it just couldn't *possibly* be anyone else. And then, when the really right man comes along, you simply can't imagine why you've been so blind and silly. I think most girls fall in love once or twice.''

"And men, too?" asked Loraine, thinking of Philip imagining that he was in love with Elinor.

"Oh, I don't doubt it," Gabrielle declared cheerfully. And Loraine thought what a darling sensible person she was, and how fortunate that nice Monsieur Florian had got her in the end.

By the time her dress was finished, Loraine could hardly believe that she was to wear anything so breathtakingly lovely. Other Florian fashions had given her infinite pleasure and pride, and the wedding dress had, in some strange way, seemed to affect her whole life. But this fancy-dress design was so rich and beautiful and becoming that it was all she could do not to lapse into some sort of pseudohistorical language to fit the picture.

Two or three days before the great evening, Gabrielle and she were taken to the theater, introduced to their two partners—both of whom came from the theater world and evidently suffered no embarrassment at finding themselves in fancy dress—and put through their paces.

It was all very exciting, and the compliments that Loraine received were gratifying in the extreme.

Only one thing cast a shadow over her enjoyment. She had heard nothing from Philip, except for one letter sent immediately after his return to London, in which he told her he had been successful in having two or three of his pictures accepted for the art show that meant so much to him.

She was delighted on his behalf, of course, and fully understood that he must be a good deal absorbed in his own affairs. But he must know that she was anxious to know just when he was returning.

Inevitably Florian inquired presently whether all her arrangements were complete. And when he heard that Philip was still in London, he was extremely annoyed.

"But this is absurd! The whole affair, planned to the last detail, is only forty-eight hours away, and you tell me we still do not know if our party is complete."

"He will come, Monsieur Florian. Of *course* he will come," Loraine insisted, for the idea that Philip could fail her was not to be entertained for one moment. "But in any case," she pointed out timidly, "for the exhibition part of the evening everything is arranged. There is no doubt about my partner for the minuet, and this is the really important—"

"Certainly not, since this I have arranged myself," interrupted Florian curtly. "I do not leave these matters in doubt. But my party, too, has been most carefully chosen and arranged, Loraine. I do not expect its balance to be upset by a wallflower, however charming."

"Oh, *monsieur*, it will be all right, I assure you." The prospective wallflower spoke with humiliated emphasis. "But—but perhaps you were right in saying that I should ask my guardian to be available, just in case."

"It is too late." Florian frowned, as though recalling that even his advice on this had been flouted.

"Too late, *monsieur*?" Loraine was taken aback. "How do you mean?"

"Monsieur Cardine is going elsewhere that evening."

"How do you know?" inquired Loraine with uncontrollable curiosity.

"Mademoiselle Roye was in here only this afternoon—"

"Elinor was?" gasped Loraine.

"—and when I asked her if she was going to the fête, she explained that she was spending the evening with her fiancé—with Monsieur Paul."

"She," Loraine swallowed, "said that? She called him her fiancé?"

"Should she not have done so?" inquired Florian, fixing Loraine with a cold glance that suggested she was trying to shift the conversation onto less vital matters.

"Oh—oh, no," said Loraine unhappily.

"Well, then, you see it is too late to secure your guardian for the evening, since you ignored my earlier advice." She had not seen Florian so angry with her since she had defied him on the opening day of the new collection. "You had better make what arrangements you can to make sure of Monsieur Philippe."

"Yes, Monsieur Florian," Loraine said meekly. And on the way home she sent a long, expensive and rather desperate telegram to Philip at the London hotel from which he had sent his earlier letter.

Then she went on home—to the chilling discovery that Paul was unexpectedly out for the evening. Mimi seemed to know very little about where he was, and Loraine could only suppose that he and Elinor had made some last-minute arrangement together.

She dined alone, feeling extremely forlorn, and with a slow resentment growing in her heart.

It was abominable of Philip to have left her in this predicament. Even if he came in the end—which of course he would do—he had absolutely no right to leave her in this state of anxiety. He must know how important it was to her to feel that everything was secure. There were some things. . . .

What was it Paul had said? There were some things that needed to be put into words. It was neither admirable nor kind to leave them in doubt.

How right! And how exactly that demonstrated the difference between Paul and Philip.

She was shocked as soon as she had allowed that

thought to invade her mind. But it recurred perpetually during the long, lonely, anxious evening.

Paul would never, never have left her in this doubt and anxiety. With Philip it was not entirely out of character. There had always, she remembered reluctantly, been a charming unpredictable quality about him. And tonight the unpredictability seemed distressingly in evidence, while it was difficult to remember the full degree of charm that had always seemed to accompany it before.

From time to time she consoled herself with the thought that she would feel better when Paul came in. But in the end he was so late that she had to go to bed before his return, and she did not see him until the next morning at breakfast.

Even then he was a little late. Which was perhaps just as well, for she would have found it hard to conceal her deep chagrin and disappointment when there was neither a letter nor a telegram from Philip.

It was a brief and silent meal on both sides, and she left for the dress house, dreading the moment when Florian would once more ask her about Philip.

Fortunately, however, he was very busy during the day. And either he forgot—a very, very unlikely circumstance, Loraine was bound to admit to herself—or else he assumed that his previous sharp words had been sufficient for her to make doubly certain that Philip would be there.

But what else could she do? She was not even sure that he was still at the hotel where she had sent the telegram. Humiliated, but not daring to let the smallest chance go by, she sent another telegram to his home address, even though she knew that Mrs. Otway was almost bound to see it.

I'll never forgive him! she told herself, hardly even noticing that it was her romantic adored Philip of whom she was thinking these hard thoughts. *To think that I relied on him, and he has put me in this ridiculous and odious position. What a way to treat anyone!*

Still there was no word from him when she reached home. And if she had not had Florian's word for it that it was Elinor with whom Paul was engaged the following evening, she would have descended to the last depths of wounded pride and begged him to put off his appointment and help her out of her predicament.

He was going out that evening, too, it seemed. This time to an official reception, however, and he kindly offered to take Loraine, too—perhaps because he noticed her blank expression when she found she was to spend the evening alone again.

However, Loraine felt it was vital to be at home and available, just in case there was any word from Philip. After all, he might well arrive in Paris that evening, having received neither of her telegrams and a good deal surprised to find she had ever doubted his coming.

This thought served to keep up her spirits for the earlier part of the evening. But when it became obvious that Philip could not be in Paris—and she had confirmed the fact by several unsuccessful telephone calls to his flat—angry resignation once more settled down upon her.

She had had strict injunctions from Madame Moisant to go to bed early, and gracious permission to arrive late at the salon next morning. So she followed out this arrangement scrupulously, though she could not resist rushing out in her dressing gown to see if the morning post had brought any letter from Philip.

There was nothing for her. And with this last deferment of hope she very nearly broke down and told Paul about her troubles.

He, however, was evidently a good deal absorbed by something that had arrived by post for him, and hardly seemed to notice the forlorn figure in the blue-flowered dressing gown who sat down opposite him and poured out coffee and crumbled a roll without eating much of it.

"Well, my dear—" he rose to go in less than ten minutes "—enjoy yourself this evening. I'm sure it will be a great occasion. I shan't see you again beforehand, shall I?''

"No. Madame Florian and I are both changing at the salon, so that every last detail can be checked, and then she has kindly asked me back to dinner at their apartment.''

"Remember all the details for me. I shall expect a blow-by-blow account later,'' he told her. And she managed to smile quite brightly as she bade him goodbye.

But when she was finally left sitting at the breakfast table alone, she almost wished that Florian had never chosen her to attend the great Fête du Roi Soleil. It hardly seemed worth all this anxiety and frustration.

And then, just when hopes were lowest and spirits most chilled, there was a sharp rap on the front door, and a minute later Mimi entered, bearing the longed-for telegram.

"Mimi!" Loraine almost snatched it from the housekeeper in her eagerness, and her fingers trembled so that she tore the sheet of paper as she dragged it out of the envelope. Then she smoothed it out and read:

A thousand regrest, darling. Cannot possibly make it tonight. Vital discussion over pictures. Have a wonderful time.

Love, Philip

CHAPTER TWELVE

HAVE A WONDERFUL TIME!

That was the sentence that fanned the flame of Loraine's anger to a degree she would not have thought possible. And in that flame there was finally consumed the last loving illusion about Philip Otway.

Have a wonderful time! What sort of time did he suppose she was likely to have, without an escort, without an explanation to give to Monsieur Florian and without a grain of real or loving regret to arm her against the bitter disappointment?

In that moment she hardly knew which caused the greater pain and disillusionment—the immediate crisis or the discovery of Philip's feet of clay.

He didn't care—that was the truth. Neither about her spoiled happiness nor her wounded pride. Nor, she saw it now, about her personally. If he had really had any tenderness or regard for her, he simply could not have done this to her. Or, if his most vital interests had absolutely demanded his presence in London, he would have found *some* way of preparing her and consoling her.

The explanation—such as it was—did not *have* to be left to the very last minute like this. The fact was that he had probably just forgotten about the whole thing in the pleasant excitement of his own affairs, and been reluctantly reminded by one or both of her telegrams.

How she wished she had never sent those telegrams. Oh, *how* she wished it! She would so much rather he should have had the impression that he was of no importance to her.

He *was* of no importance now. Astounding, unbelievable discovery—but true. In a matter of days he had slipped completely from his pedestal and now, revealed in the light of his own selfish telegram, he appeared as he really was.

Charming and friendly to a degree. But none of it was more than skin-deep. Carelessly generous when it cost him nothing and the result was a pleasing degree of gratitude and hero worship. But in the final event there was really only one person who meant a great deal to him and whose interests he was ready to study. And that was the handsome, gifted, easygoing Philip Otway himself.

With disconcerting clarity, Loraine remembered now one occasion after another when he had really shown quite obviously what he was. And, oddly enough, what she remembered most clearly of all at that moment was the casual way he had shrugged off Elinor Roye, once he had no more use for her.

I should have seen then that he was essentially cold-hearted, Loraine thought. *Poor Elinor! Now I can feel truly sorry for her.*

But then, with a shock that was almost physical, she remembered that she had no reason to feel sorry for Elinor at all. On the contrary. The shoe was on the other foot, if anything. Elinor had emerged from all this exceedingly well, as the fiancée of Paul once more.

Oh, lucky, lucky Elinor! How wonderfully different was her fate. She was to marry Paul, who was—even without the comparison with the erring Philip to highlight the fact—a prince among men.

He had never left any vital matter casually in doubt. On the contrary, he had defined her position beyond question, when he had categorically said that his home was hers for as long as she wished.

Not that she could impose on that generous declaration too far, of course. But oh, how she loved him for it!

It was the nicest thing that ever happened to me, thought Loraine with a sigh. *That and the way he looked at me when I wore the wedding dress.*

But this was no time to idle away the few hours left in nostalgic recollection. Philip had presented her with an immediate problem. And the only way of solving it was to go straight to Florian and frankly admit that he had been right and she had been wrong.

It was not a pleasant prospect. But without knowing it, Loraine had grown up fast in the past painful half hour and her scale of values had changed subtly. No longer was she the timid girl prepared to make a worrying mountain out of a social molehill. She was beginning to know now what really mattered and what did not.

If Monsieur Florian chose to be cross with her, that would serve her right and she must accept the fact. But it was inconceivable that he would really find the problem a serious one. On such an occasion, the difficulty would be not to find an extra man to complete his party but to decide which of many he would choose.

And so, plucking up her courage, Loraine went to the telephone and dialed Monsieur Florian's private number.

Her heart beat apprehensively as she waited for the reply. But then it was Gabrielle's sweet warm voice that answered her.

"I'm sorry, my dear. He's just gone to the salon. Is there anything I can do for you?" she asked.

"Well, it's really something for Monsieur Florian himself to deal with, and he's going to be very cross with me, I expect," Loraine admitted. "My escort for the evening has let me down." She had no idea she was already speaking in entirely different terms from those she would have used if Philip had still been the man in her life. "Monsieur Florian warned me to have a substitute in readiness, and I'm afraid I ignored the warning."

"I shouldn't worry." Gabrielle was eminently reassuring. "Georges will soon rustle up someone. How do you like them? Young and gay, or older and interesting?"

Loraine laughed and immediately felt better.

"I don't really mind, as long as Monsieur Florian doesn't feel I've spoiled his party."

"Of course not!" Gabrielle scouted the notion. "I'll phone him now. I'm sorry about your disappointment. Was it someone very special?"

There was a second's pause. Then Loraine said quite deliberately, "Not really—no. He was charming but rather lightweight and not particularly important to me."

"Oh, good. Well, we'll find you someone nice. I'll get on to Georges now and tell him to do his stuff."

So Loraine replaced the receiver, feeling that her immediate problem was in good hands. And, indeed, by the time she arrived at the salon, Georges had evidently done his stuff to some purpose, for, meeting Loraine on the stairs, he said quite agreeably, "I have found you an escort for tonight, *petite*. Don't worry."

"Oh, thank you, *monsieur*! I'm sorry I was silly and didn't take your advice before."

"Which of us does take advice if it runs contrary to our wishes?" replied Florian good-humoredly. "Would it be tactless to inquire what happened to Monsieur Philippe?"

"He stayed in London, *monsieur*, and sent me a very casual telegram of regrets," replied Loraine with courageous candor.

"Tch, tch," said Florian, in high good humor—presumably at the vindication of his own views. "That was neither polite nor kind of him."

"That's what I thought," agreed Loraine with a touch of bitterness that made Florian regard his youngest model with unusual attention.

"*Chérie*, we all have to grow up," he said kindly, "and part of the process is nearly always painful. But console yourself, for remember that your basic instinct was singularly correct."

"My basic instinct, *monsieur*?" Loraine, who was not feeling particularly proud of her instinct just then, looked surprised. "What do you mean? When, for goodness' sake, did I show wise basic instinct?"

"On the opening day of the new collection. Remember? 'I didn't look at Philip, after all. I looked at Paul.' "

And smiling a little to himself Florian passed on, leaving Loraine to gaze after him with a startled expression.

For almost half a minute she stood there on the famous staircase. Then she went on slowly up to her own floor, in a great confusion of mind.

Florian, of course, was oversimplifying things. He was also, apparently, overlooking Elinor's part in the general picture. What if—just for the sake of argument—some inner wiser self *had* prompted her to look at Paul on that great occasion? The practical result amounted to very little.

Paul and she were simply guardian and ward. Devoted guardian and ward, it was true, during recent weeks. But that was hardly a relationship that carried any element of romance.

Or did it?

"Loraine...attention, please!" Madame Moisant's sharp voice recalled her to humdrum reality. "To be allowed to come late is already a privilege. To go to the fête tonight may make you feel important. But neither of these privileges entitles you to ignore me when I speak to you."

"Oh, *madame*, I didn't mean to!" Loraine was immediately contrite. "I'm sorry. I think I was just in a brown study."

"Dreaming of the prince or count or whoever it is that Monsieur Florian has secured for her tonight," jeered Lisette. "Too bad that your own beau preferred not to go with you after all."

"That will do, Lisette." Madame Moisant, who could scold with energy, had really rather a soft spot for Loraine and came to her aid immediately. "This is no business of yours. You have been eavesdropping as usual, I suppose, and misinterpreted what you heard.

Loraine is the guest of Monsieur Florian tonight. You may envy her if you wish, but not insult her."

Lisette lapsed into silence. But she could not resist one or two other pinpricks during the day. To her surprise, however, Loraine found that they caused her singularly little unhappiness, which was, she supposed, the full measure of her cure.

Incredible though it might seem, she no longer cared that Philip had stayed in London. In a curious way, what had loomed as a major tragedy yesterday was now shrinking to the proportions of a minor inconvenience. And even that Monsieur Florian had now set right.

Late in the afternoon Gabrielle arrived, and she and Loraine were arrayed in all their festive finery and allowed to parade for the inspection of all. Loud were the exclamations of praise and congratulation, and indescribably smug and satisfied the expressions of those who had actually been responsible for the making of the dresses.

Then Florian swept them both off in his car, and Loraine felt that the full glory of the evening had begun.

She wished Paul could have seen her, for no description, however detailed, could give any idea of the beauty of her dress. But thinking about him made her recall that he was going out with Elinor instead, and somehow that made her feel so unhappy that she tried to think of something else. Leaning forward from the back seat of the car, she asked, "Whom did you choose for my escort in the end, Monsieur Florian?"

"A very good friend of mine." Florian spoke briefly over his shoulder, most of his attention on the madly speeding traffic. "I think you will like him and find him a satisfactory substitute for Monsieur Philippe."

Then he resumed some discussion with his wife, and she found she could not ask any further details. But she sat back and relaxed; she could wait for those until the moment of introduction.

Loraine had never been to the Florians' apartment before and was, like everyone else before her, enchanted by its beautiful position at the top of a high luxury block, with breathtaking views of Paris from every window.

Gabrielle took her to a charming bedroom and left her there, with instructions to go into the drawing room when she was ready, as Georges would be looking after the drinks there, and she herself had one or two last-minute instructions to give in connection with the small dinner party to be given before the evening's festivities.

Loraine completed her few running repairs in a leisurely way and then stood by the window for a while, watching the first faint veils of summer dusk gathering over Paris.

What a beautiful city it was! And how many things had happened to her in the months she had been here. She had come as a wide-eyed unknowing schoolgirl. And here she had experienced romance and heartache, found her place in a glamorous competitive world—and come to know the dearest, most worthwhile person she would ever meet.

Half charmed, half scared, she found it was Paul who dominated the picture as she looked back. Paul, remote and chilling when he met her at the station, startled and moved when she had put her cheek against his arm and coaxed him to let her go to work at Florian's. Paul telling her that her capacity for enjoying herself was a delicious discovery for him. Paul teasing her, consoling her, encouraging her, reassuring her that his home was hers. Paul rising to his feet and murmuring, "You darling!" as she passed him in the wedding dress.

Insensibly, he had become so much a part of her life and her daily joy, and she had taken it all for granted. As one took the sun for granted, or the lovely miracle of the twilight moving softly across the city now, as she stood looking down upon it.

I can't imagine life without him, she thought in sudden panic. *I—I couldn't bear it.*

And because the discovery and all its implications terrified her, she thrust it from her and, turning from the window, went quickly from the room. She would find Florian and let him give her a stiff drink, and tomorrow she would worry about the fearful new problem that was already casting its shadow upon her.

A little breathlessly she entered the long lovely drawing room with windows at both ends. And because the setting sun was shining into the room she was dazzled at first and thought the man standing by the window must be Florian.

Then he turned. And it was not Florian at all. It was Paul.

For a moment she almost thought she must have conjured him up in person by the sheer intensity of her thoughts and her feelings. But then the absolute joy of his presence swept everything else aside, and she cried, "Paul—Paul darling!" and ran to him.

"Loraine," he laughed, caught her up in his arms and kissed her once or twice with the utmost tenderness. "What a delightful welcome."

"Oh, but I'm so glad—so happy! It's the most wonderful surprise. How did you come here?"

"Florian asked me to be your escort for the evening."

"Oh, but you were going out with Elinor, weren't you?"

He shook his head and smiled.

"What gave you that idea?"

"Florian told me you were."

An odd look came over Paul's face at that, and he said gravely, "Even Florian makes a mistake sometimes."

"But he was so positive. He said Elinor told him. Oh, it doesn't matter, of course. Only—" a twinge of conscience invaded the security of her happiness "—you aren't just letting her down, are you? I know what that feels like."

"No, darling. That isn't my way of doing things. And since this seems to be one of those things that needs exact definition, the last time I went out with Elinor was the evening you and Philip visited our restaurant. We had a frank discussion that ended in our deciding there was no point in our seeing each other again."

"But you said—when I asked you if it had been a satisfactory evening—you said it had been very satisfactory."

"From my point of view, it was," he informed her with a dry smile. "That was another situation that I wanted clearly defined."

"You mean you didn't *want* to see her again?"

"I mean I didn't want to see her again. Or rather, that it was a matter of indifference to me whether we ran into each other or not, but that I had no intention of arranging any meeting."

"Paul!" She looked at him in incredulous delight. "Wasn't this all very sudden?"

"No."

"But—" she frowned in an effort to recall what had left her with the complete conviction that he had continued to love Elinor and rejoiced when she was free again "—but when I told you that the engagement between Philip and Elinor was broken, you agreed that was the thing you had most wanted to hear."

"We both put it in the past, darling," he reminded her. "It *was* once the thing I most wanted to hear. For some time it had already ceased to be so."

"Oh, Paul—" she gave a smiling, reproachful little shake of her head "—you did give me a lot of wrong impressions quite deliberately, didn't you?"

"What else can a man do when the girl he adores insists on telling him she's in love with someone else?" he countered smilingly.

"When the girl he.... Paul!" Her hand tightened suddenly on his arm. "S-say that again."

He laughed softly and kissed the side of her cheek, just where the excited color was beginning to deepen.

"Suppose I say it in another form," he suggested teasingly. "What else could I do when my heart's darling kept on telling me she was in love with Philip Otway?"

"Paul!"

She put her head down against his shoulder, and for a long moment nothing and no one else existed. Not Paris, Philip, Florian, the fête, Elinor—anything. All she knew was that she was safe and that everything was all right.

Paul loved her and his arms were around her. The rest of the world, and all her life, could wait while she savored the perfection of that magic moment. Paul loved her and she was safe in his arms.

Then at last she said wonderingly, "*Am* I your heart's darling?"

"Yes, Loraine."

"Will you think me silly and shallow and changeable if I tell you that you're mine, too?"

"No, my darling. That's the thing I most want to hear now. So you see, I, too, must admit that I've undergone a great change. You're not alone in that."

"Oh, Paul, you do have the most comforting things to say!" She hugged him gratefully. "Almost anyone else would tease me and make me feel small."

"I love you," he reminded her simply. "I don't want you to feel small. I like you to feel and look wonderful. That time I saw you in the wedding dress—"

"Oh, *then*! That was the moment," she exclaimed in delight. "That was when *it* really happened to both of us, whether we knew it or not. Oh, clever, clever Monsieur Florian!"

And as though on his cue, Florian came into the room at that point and smilingly asked, "What have I done to evoke this charming tribute, *ma chère*?"

"I'm sure you know," Loraine laughed across at him in her happiness. "And although I suspect that you told one thumping lie in order to achieve your purpose, I think I must forgive you. You always backed Paul to marry me, didn't you?"

"At least I felt that my wedding dress would be sadly wasted if Monsieur Philippe succeeded," the great designer admitted dryly.

"It was not wasted," Loraine told him with a smile. "Remember? I didn't look at Philip, after all. I looked at Paul."

"I remember."

"What's this all about?" inquired Paul, looking amused and intrigued.

"Loraine will tell you in detail another time," Florian assured him. "I think I hear our other guests arriving, just in time to drink a toast to our newly engaged pair."

And even as he spoke Gabrielle entered, accompanied, to Loraine's most genuine pleasure, by Marianne and Roger Senloe.

"Dear Florian." Marianne kissed his cheek lightly, while Roger shook him warmly by the hand. "Not matchmaking again, surely? This is becoming a habit."

"A habit that you should be the last to deplore, my dear Marianne," retorted Florian, handing around glasses.

"I don't deplore it. As a satisfied client, I'm interested, that's all." Marianne laughed and looked with kindly curiosity upon her onetime bridesmaid.

"An engagement? This is the first I've heard of it," Gabrielle exclaimed. "Is this really an engagement party?"

"Loraine's and mine," Paul explained, drawing Loraine into the circle of his arm.

"But how lovely!" Gabrielle kissed Loraine impulsively. Then she raised her glass and said, "To you both, my dears!"

"To the matchmaker!" added Marianne, raising her glass mockingly in Florian's direction.

But with a reflective smile Florian disclaimed the tribute.

"To the wedding dress," he said. "The symbol of our art—and of the magic that each one of us here has found."

Great old favorites...
Harlequin Classic Library

The **HARLEQUIN CLASSIC LIBRARY**
is offering some of the best in romance fiction—
great old classics from our early publishing lists.

Complete and mail this coupon today!

Harlequin Reader Service

In U.S.A. 1440 South Priest Drive
Tempe, AZ 85281

In Canada 649 Ontario Street
Stratford, Ontario N5A 6W2

Please send me the following novels from the Harlequin Classic Library. I am enclosing my check or money order for $1.50 for each novel ordered, plus 75¢ to cover postage and handling. If I order all nine titles at one time, I will receive a FREE book, *Calling Nurse Blair,* by Lucy Agnes Hancock.

☐ 73 **Orphan Bride**
   Sara Seale

☐ 74 **The Tender Bond**
   Jill Christian

☐ 75 **Heatherleigh**
   Essie Summers

☐ 76 **Portrait of Susan**
   Rosalind Brett

☐ 77 **Pilgrim Heart**
   Vivian Stuart

☐ 78 **Gates of Dawn**
   Susan Barrie

☐ 79 **The Black Cameron**
   Jean S. MacLeod

☐ 80 **The Doctor's Daughters**
   Anne Weale

☐ 81 **The Golden Peaks**
   Eleanor Farnes

Number of novels checked @ $1.50 each =	$ _____
N.Y. and Ariz. residents add appropriate sales tax	$ _____
Postage and handling	$ _____ .75
TOTAL $ _____

I enclose _____
(Please send check or money order. We cannot be responsible for cash sent through the mail.)

Prices subject to change without notice.

Name _____
         (Please Print)

Address _____

City _____

State/Prov. _____ Zip/Postal Code _____